Memories of the attack assailed her.

As she dragged in a breath of fresh air, her head pounded. Overhead, geese honked. If only she could fly away from the chaos like the geese.

Movement caught her eye at the edge of the woods. An animal? Or—

She recognized the danger almost too late. Her heart lurching, she ran for the protection of her house. She tripped and fell as a sound exploded and a flowerpot shattered beside her.

Another shot, and then another.

She scrambled for the door, and Zach was there, pulling her inside to safety, his arms sure and comforting. He pulled her to the floor and slammed the door. "Stay down."

"A man. In the woods. He had a rifle."

She saw the tension on his face, and the realization made her tremble with fear. Last night an intruder had broken into her clinic. Today that intruder became a killer.

And the person he wanted to kill was her.

Debby Giusti is an award-winning Christian author who met and married her military husband at Fort Knox, Kentucky. Together they traveled the world, raised three wonderful children and have now settled in Atlanta, Georgia, where Debby spins tales of mystery and suspense that touch the heart and soul. Visit Debby online at debbygiusti.com, blog with her at seekerville.blogspot.com and craftieladiesofromance.blogspot.com, and email her at Debby@DebbyGiusti.com.

Books by Debby Giusti

Love Inspired Suspense

Military Investigations

The Officer's Secret
The Captain's Mission
The Colonel's Daughter
The General's Secretary
The Soldier's Sister
The Agent's Secret Past
Stranded
Person of Interest
Plain Danger
Plain Truth

Visit the Author Profile page at Harlequin.com for more titles.

PLAIN TRUTH

DEBBY GIUSTI

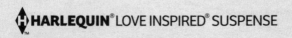

HARLEQUIN® LOVE INSPIRED® SUSPENSE

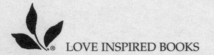 LOVE INSPIRED BOOKS

Recycling programs for this product may not exist in your area.

ISBN-13: 978-0-373-44766-4

Plain Truth

Copyright © 2016 by Deborah W. Giusti

www.Harlequin.com

Printed in U.S.A.

People were bringing children to Jesus
that He might touch them, but the disciples rebuked them.
When Jesus saw this He became indignant and said to
them, "Let the children come to me; do not prevent them,
for the kingdom of God belongs to such as these. Amen, I
say to you, whoever does not accept the kingdom of God
like a child will not enter it." Then He embraced them
and blessed them, placing His hands on them.
–Mark 10:13-16

This book is dedicated to my wonderful grandchildren,
Anna, Robert, John Anthony and William.
You fill my heart with joy!

ONE

Dr. Ella Jacobsen startled with fright as a crash of thunder shook her rural medical clinic. Dropping the invitation she'd been reading for the upcoming medical symposium onto her desk, she glanced out the window as another bolt of lightning lit the night sky. Anticipating the power outage that would surely follow, Ella pulled the Maglite from the bottom drawer of her file cabinet and sighed with frustration as the lights flicked off, leaving her in darkness and fumbling with the switch on the flashlight.

If someone had warned her about how often she'd lose electricity, she might have chosen another location for the pediatric clinic. As it was, after five months, she was committed to the rural farm community near Freemont, Georgia, and to her patients, two of whom had just received IV fluids in her treatment room.

Relieved when the Maglite finally switched on, she followed the arc of light through her clinic to the hallway and peered into the room where the five-year-old twins rested comfortably. Their worry-worn mother, Mary Kate Powers, slept on the chair next to the girls, oblivious to the pummeling rain and howling wind outside.

Ella wouldn't disturb the young mother's sleep. Instead, she slipped into her slicker and left her clinic through the side door, heading for the generator that provided a backup power source.

Quin would have called her generator inadequate, but her deceased husband had been prone to point out any number of her shortcomings. Surely eight months after his death was time enough to cease worrying about what Quin thought.

Ella grimaced as the storm exploded around her. Lightning bolted overhead, followed almost instantly by ear-shattering thunder. Rain fell in torrents, stinging her face and drenching her hair. Too late, she pulled the hood of her coat over her head and bent into the wind as she picked her way through the sodden grass to the generator.

Tonight, the tin overhang that usually provided protection from the elements did little to stem the battering rain and buffeting wind. She grabbed the gas can out of the nearby shed and filled the generator's tank before she flipped the fuel valve to On and pulled out the choke. After pressing the control switch, she grabbed the pull cord and yanked once, then twice.

The engine failed to engage.

She tugged on the cord again and again, then sighed.

A sound caused her to turn. Through the downpour, she watched the headlights of a car race along the two-lane road in front of her property. For half a heartbeat, she wanted to flag down the driver and beg for help. Then she steeled her shoulders and shoved out her chin with resolve. She'd come this far alone, and she wouldn't waver in her determination to succeed. Although, in spite of her attempt to be self-reliant, a sinking feeling settled in the pit of her stomach as the car disappeared from sight.

Another bolt of lightning flashed across the sky. In the yard, the sign for the Children's Care Clinic snapped in the wind. She was alone, other than for an exhausted mother and her two daughters in the building. Like it or not, Ella needed to solve her own problems.

Opening the oil cap, she checked the level, making certain it was adequate. Then, after adjusting the choke, she pulled on the cord again…and again…and again.

Her hand cramped with the effort. Stopping to catch her breath, she stretched her fingers and listened to a sound that floated over the storm.

Turning her gaze toward the clinic, she tilted her head as the sound came again.

Was it a cry? No, a scream!

Her heart lurched.

Grabbing the Maglite, she hurried across the slippery, rain-wet grass. Her shoes sank into a patch of Georgia red clay that grabbed like quicksand. Pulling free, she raced to the side door, shook the rain from her hair and stepped inside. Before she was halfway across the office, she stopped short. Someone else was in the room. She narrowed her gaze and raised her flashlight.

A figure bathed in shadow stood over her desk. He raised an even more powerful light that blinded her in its glare. Momentarily frozen in place, she failed to react as he raced toward her and grabbed her shoulder. The crushing strength of his hold made her legs buckle. She dropped to the floor, losing her Maglite in the fall, and crawled on hands and knees to escape his hold.

He kicked her side. She collapsed. He kicked again.

Air whooshed from her lungs.

She rolled over, and caught his foot before he could strike a third blow. Twisting his leg, she forced him off balance.

He cursed.

She grabbed his thigh above his knee and dug her nails into the tender flesh. He raised his right hand. She scooted sideways to avoid the strike, but her reflexes weren't fast enough. His fist made contact with her neck, below her ear. Her body arched with pain.

His shadowed bulk loomed above her. He drew a weapon from his pocket, aimed and squeezed the trigger.

She screamed, expecting to be killed.

The bullet failed to discharge. Again he tried. And again.

Lightning slashed outside, but all she saw was the glare of his flashlight and the gun that refused to fire.

He growled like an animal, a monster who wanted her dead. Raising his hand, he hurled the weapon against her skull. She screamed in pain, then slipped into darkness, surrounded by a cushion of oblivion.

Thoughts of her patients dragged her back to reality. She blinked her eyes open and listened to his footsteps moving away from her. A door slammed, then another wave of oblivion overtook her. When she came to, panic grabbed at her throat. Worried about Mary Kate and the girls, she knew she had to get help.

Ella inched toward the desk, where she'd left her cell phone. Her head and neck ached. Nausea washed over her. She raised herself far enough off the floor to grab her cell, tapped in 911 and turned to glance over her shoulder, using the light from her phone to scan the darkness.

A body.

No. Please, God, no.

Mary Kate lay in a pool of blood.

"Nine one one." The operator's raspy voice sounded in the stillness. "State your emergency."

"Children's Care Clinic on Amish Road." Ella gripped the phone with her trembling hand and forced the words from her mouth. "An…an intruder attacked two women. Send an ambulance."

"Ma'am, could you—"

Scooting closer, she gasped at the gush of blood from

the young woman's side. Grabbing a towel from the nearby supply cabinet, Ella wadded it into a ball and pressed the thick terry cloth against the wound. With her right hand, she found the carotid artery, grateful to feel a pulse.

"Tell the ambulance to hurry," she told the operator. "I've got a patient who's bleeding to death."

"Stay on the line, ma'am. The police and ambulance are on the way."

Ella wasn't sure they would arrive in time.

Criminal Investigation Division Special Agent Zach Swain stood at the side entrance of the rural clinic that led into the doctor's office and blinked back the memory of another medical facility long ago. A patient lay sprawled on the floor, and a doctor knelt over her, forcing air into her lungs. Fear clenched his gut as he was once again the eight-year-old boy screaming for the doctor to save his mother's life.

Swallowing down the vision from his past, Zach focused on the swirl of activity before him and the information Officer Van Taylor, a young Freemont cop who had checked Zach's identification, was continuing to provide.

"Her name's Ella Jacobsen." Taylor, tall and lean and midtwenties, pointed to the woman sitting on a straight-backed chair.

"She runs the clinic?" Zach asked.

The cop nodded. "She bought the three-bedroom ranch and attached a clinic to the side of the residence. Local families and some of the Amish who've settled in this area appreciate having a doc close at hand."

An older police sergeant, probably fifty-five, with a receding hairline and bushy brows, stood near the woman. Zach read his name tag: Abrams. The sergeant held an open notebook in his hand.

Zach couldn't hear their conversation, but he recognized the ashen paleness of the doctor's face and the bloodstains that covered her blouse and the slicker that lay next to her on the floor.

"She's a northerner," the younger officer explained. "Moved here from Pennsylvania and opened this clinic for kids five months ago."

All of which sounded admirable. "So what happened tonight?" Zach asked.

"The power went out, only it wasn't the storm that caused the failure."

Zach raised his brow. "Someone tampered with the line coming to the clinic?"

"Seems that's what happened. He also fiddled with the spark plug on the generator the doc couldn't get to start. One of our men got it working until the repairman from the power company restored the main feed."

"I call that good customer service this far from Freemont."

Taylor leaned closer and lowered his voice. "The guy on call from the power company is married to Sergeant Abrams's daughter, so he rushed here to help."

"Keep it in the family, right?"

The young cop smiled. "In case you're interested, we took the doc's prints and collected samples from under her nails."

Which meant she had tried to defend herself.

Taylor pointed to his supervisor. "Looks like the sergeant is ready to wrap up his questioning, sir, if you want to talk to Dr. Jacobsen."

Zach nodded in appreciation.

Abrams closed his notebook, said something to the woman and then headed across the room. As he approached, Zach extended his hand and stated his name. "I'm with the Criminal Investigation Division at Fort Rickman, Sergeant Abrams. One of your men notified our office that active duty military personnel were involved in the case."

The sergeant returned the handshake. "Good to see you, Special Agent Swain. What we know so far is that an intruder attacked Mary Kate Powers, whose twin girls were being treated by the doctor. The woman's a military spouse. She suffered a gunshot wound to her side and is being transported by ambulance to the hospital at Fort Rickman. Doc Jacobsen tended to her injuries before the EMTs arrived. Saved the woman's life, according to our emergency personnel."

Zach glanced again at the doc's scraped face and disheveled hair. "Looks like the assailant took out his anger on the doctor, as well."

"She claims to be all right, although she can't remember much. Probably due to shock."

"Do you have a motive?"

The sergeant shrugged. "Could be drugs. The doc doesn't keep much on hand in her clinic, but dopers don't make good choices."

"Was the assailant able to access the meds?"

"Negative. Still, that seems the most logical explanation at this point."

Logical or convenient? Zach wasn't as easily convinced as the sergeant. "Mind if I talk to her?"

"Be my guest. Corporal Hugh Powers, the wounded woman's husband, is in one of the treatment rooms. You're welcome to question him, as well."

Zach appreciated the cop's openness to having a military presence in the investigation. As the sergeant and Taylor stepped outside, Zach grabbed a chair and placed it next to the doctor.

She glanced up. Blue eyes rimmed with dark lashes stared at him. Her brow furrowed, and her full lips drooped into a pronounced frown. She scooted back in her chair warily.

Zach introduced himself. "I'm from Fort Rickman. If you don't mind, I'd like to ask you a few questions."

"I don't understand." Her hand went protectively to her throat. "Why would Fort Rickman be interested in what happened at my clinic?"

Zach eyed the dark mark under her ear and the hair on the side of her head that was matted with blood. "The Criminal Investigations Division is called in when military personnel are injured or involved in a crime."

"You're referring to Mary Kate?"

"That's right. Mary Kate Powers. You were treating her daughters?"

The doc nodded. "They were suffering from a gastrointestinal problem and became dehydrated. I administered IV fluids to rehydrate the girls."

"Were they in the clinic at the time of the attack?"

"They were asleep, as was their mother." Ella pointed to the hallway. "The girls were in the first treatment room, on the left. Their stepfather got here before the ambulance. He wanted to check on his wife, since she and the girls had been gone quite a while. He was distraught when he saw her, of course, and called the grandparents. They arrived not long ago and took the children home."

"Am I correct in assuming the girls weren't injured?"

"Thankfully, they slept through their mother's attack."

"Could you start at the beginning, ma'am?"

She glanced down at her scraped hands. Dried blood stained her fingers. Rust-colored spatters streaked across her shirt. "I've been treating the girls for a debilitating disease, called CED, or childhood enzyme deficiency, for the last few months. They've improved, but when the gastrointestinal problems started, their mother was concerned. She called and asked if I could see them tonight."

"Was this a normal occurrence, Doctor?"

She narrowed her gaze as if she didn't understand the question. "If you mean do I see patients at night, then no, it's not the norm. But the girls are five years old, Mr. Swain. Their physical and fine motor abilities had been compromised by the disease. Less than two months ago, I was worried about their failure to thrive."

"You didn't expect them to live?"

She nodded. "They were becoming increasingly compromised."

"But you recognized the symptoms and started them on the proper medication?" Zach asked.

"More or less."

Now he was the one to pause and raise an eyebrow. "Meaning what?"

"Meaning my husband led the team that first identified the condition. I called the research center where he had worked to ensure the protocol he established almost a year ago was still the treatment of choice."

"And was it?"

"Yes, so after talking to the head of the Harrisburg center, I made changes in the girls' diets, prescribed the enzyme needed to overcome their deficiency and checked on their progress repeatedly."

"The girls improved?"

The doc nodded. "Improved and indeed began to thrive."

"Yet they got sick with the stomach ailment."

"Which had nothing to do with the genetic disease. As you can imagine, their mother was anxious. I assured her the girls would be fine with fluids and time. Antinausea drugs helped. I'll check on them again in the morning, but I feel sure they'll make a full recovery."

The doctor glanced at an area near her desk where blood stained the tile floor. "I wish I was equally as convinced of their mother's prognosis."

"You don't think she'll survive?" Zach asked.

"Mary Kate lost a lot of blood. A whole host of complications could develop. The next twenty-four to forty-eight hours will be key."

"Why would someone harm Mrs. Powers?"

The doc shook her head, a bit too quickly.

Zach leaned closer. "Is there someone who might have reason to attack the girls' mother?"

"You'd have to ask Mary Kate, although I doubt you'll be able to question her for the next day or two." Dr. Jacobsen glanced again at the floor. "Even then, I'm not sure…"

"I'll contact the hospital," Zach volunteered.

She glanced up at him, her eyes wide with hopeful optimism. "Would you let me know her condition?"

"Of course."

She almost smiled.

Zach let out a breath, checked the notes he'd made and tried to get back to his questioning. "Could you tell me about your husband, ma'am?"

"My husband?"

Any positive steps he had made took a backward dive as her frown returned.

"You mentioned that he had worked at a research center in Pennsylvania," Zach prompted. "Where is your husband currently working?"

"My husband…" She pulled in a ragged breath. "Quin died eight months ago."

Not what Zach had expected. "I'm sorry, ma'am."

"Thank you. So am I."

"You lived with him in Pennsylvania?"

"I did. That's correct."

"And after he passed away…" Zach let the statement hang.

"After his death, I moved to Georgia and opened this clinic."

"Georgia must not be home, ma'am. I don't notice a Southern accent."

She tilted her head. "I'm originally from Ohio. I met and married my husband in Columbus when I was attending medical school at Ohio State. He was doing research for a private company."

"What brought you South after his death?"

She touched the ring finger of her left hand as if searching for the wedding band she no longer wore.

"I came to Freemont because of the Amish who live in the area. Some of the families migrated here from Pennsylvania, a few from Ohio and Alabama. Seems everyone—even the 'English,' as they call us—wants a bit of the simple lifestyle. Land up north is hard to find, which forces young Amish farmers to settle new areas, away from the urban sprawl that has become a problem."

"So you were looking for an Amish community?"

"I'm a pediatrician." She sounded tired. Perhaps from too many questions. "I wanted to open a care clinic for Amish children."

"But the Powers twins aren't Amish."

"Mary Kate grew up around here. As you probably know, her husband—the girls' stepfather—is military and was deployed to the Middle East. Mary Kate and the girls moved home to be with her parents. My clinic is closer than going to town for medical treatment."

Zach studied the notes he had taken. Something didn't add up. "Your husband worked with the Amish in Pennsylvania?"

"Amish children. He specialized in newly emerging, genetically acquired diseases, as well as established conditions that impact the Amish."

"What specifically?"

"Metabolic disorders such as pyruvate kinase deficiency, Crigler-Najjar syndrome, maple syrup urine disease."

Zach held up his hand. "Evidently there are a number of conditions that attack Amish children."

"Too many. As I mentioned, Quin worked to identify new diseases and researched treatment protocols."

"Then you moved here after his death to carry on his legacy?"

"No." Confusion washed over her face. "I came because I wanted to make a contribution."

From the noticeable way she braced her shoulders and raised her head, Zach wondered if there was more to her statement than she cared to admit. Had the doctor been living in her husband's shadow?

"What was the cause of your husband's death, ma'am?"

She bristled. "I don't see how that has bearing on what happened here tonight."

"Yes, ma'am, but it's my job to put the pieces together. Your husband's death could play a role in the investigation."

"I find that hard to believe."

Zach raised his brow and waited. Dr. Jacobsen had to realize that police questions needed to be answered.

"My husband's cause of death is still under investigation," she finally admitted.

"Could you provide a few more details?"

"Quin attended a medical research conference in Memphis, Tennessee. He left the hotel Saturday afternoon before the end of the event. His luggage was in the rental car found on the edge of a bridge that spans the Mississippi River."

Her face twisted as if the story was hard to tell.

"Fishermen found his body washed up on the banks of the river some days later."

"Was foul play suspected?"

She swallowed. "The police ruled his death self-inflicted."

Suicide, but she failed to use the term. "Did you question their finding?" Zach asked.

"Of course. Anything could have happened. He could have fallen or been pushed."

"You suspected foul play?"

She shook her head. "I don't know what I suspected. Quin was a perfectionist. He held himself to a high standard. Succumbing to the sense of unworthiness that predisposes someone to take their own life hardly seemed in keeping with Quin's nature."

"Did you explain your concerns to the police?"

"They weren't interested in my opinions."

A negative undercurrent was evident from her tone of voice. Zach doubted the good doctor had much regard for law enforcement, present company included, he felt sure.

"What about tonight's assailant. Did you see anything that might identify the intruder?"

She raked her hand through her curly hair and shook her head. "I don't remember."

When Zach failed to comment, she leaned closer. "I passed out. Not long. A matter of seconds at the most, yet my recall is foggy at best."

Opening her hands, she shrugged. "The truth is I can't remember anything that happened shortly before or after I blacked out."

"What's the last thing you *do* remember, ma'am?"

"I was outside, trying to make the generator work. A scream came from the clinic. I hurried inside to make sure Mary Kate and the girls were all right."

"What did you find?"

Her eyes narrowed. "A man shadowed in darkness stood over my desk."

"Go on," Zach encouraged her.

She shook her head. "That's all I can recall."

The side door opened and Sergeant Abrams and Officer Taylor stepped back into the clinic. After saying something to the younger cop, Abrams approached the doctor. "Ma'am, the EMTs mentioned your need to be checked at the hospital. I can have one of my men drive you there in the next twenty to thirty minutes."

"That's not necessary. All I really need are a couple of ibuprofen and a few hours of sleep."

"If the Freemont police are tied up, I'd be happy to drive you to the hospital," Zach volunteered. "You've been through a lot and are probably running on adrenaline right now."

"Really, I'm fine," she insisted.

The sergeant leaned closer. "Ma'am, you owe it to your patients to be checked out. The sooner you get feeling better, the sooner you'll be able to see to their needs."

The man seemed to have struck the right chord.

"Perhaps you're right." She glanced at Zach. "You wouldn't mind driving me?"

"Not a problem, ma'am."

She looked down at her soiled hands and blouse. "If you don't mind, I'd like to wash my hands and change into clean clothes."

"Of course."

Abrams motioned a female cop forward. "Officer Grant will accompany you into your private residence, ma'am."

"But it adjoins my clinic," the doc objected. "I just need to go down the hall. The door connects to the kitchen."

"Yes, ma'am." The sergeant nodded. "But having someone with you is a safety precaution until you've been checked out at the hospital."

As if too tired to argue, Dr. Jacobsen rose and followed the female officer into the hallway.

Once the women had left the room, Zach turned to the

sergeant. "Tell me if I'm wrong, but I get the feeling you don't trust the doc."

Abrams offered him a tired smile. "I'm being cautious. Dr. Jacobsen seems to be a woman of merit, but I've seen too many criminals over the years who look like Miss America and apple pie. I don't want to be hoodwinked by a physician in a rural clinic who's up to no good."

Zach hadn't suspected the doctor of wrongdoing. Quite the opposite. He wouldn't admit his feelings to the sergeant, but something about her tugged at his heart. Maybe it was the confusion he read in her gaze, or her vulnerability. Whatever the reason, he needed to focus on the case at hand. He also needed to remind himself of what he'd learned long ago.

Ever since his mother's traumatic death, Zach didn't trust doctors. He never had and never would.

TWO

Ella stepped into the hallway and paused. Her head ached, and the muscles in her back and legs were strained. Although she'd survived the attack, her insides were still trembling. After Quin's death, she had moved to Georgia, looking for a better life. Now an intruder had robbed her of her peace and sense of security.

She doubted that the special agent could understand the way she felt. He was big and bulky, and impeccably dressed in a navy sports coat and khaki slacks, with a patterned tie that brought out his rugged complexion and dark eyes. Some might call him handsome. She found him intense.

Glancing into the small treatment room, she saw Hugh Powers, head in his hands, sitting in the chair where his wife had slept not that long ago.

Ella tapped on the door frame. "Corporal Powers?"

He glanced up.

"I'm sorry about Mary Kate."

"The EMTs said she would have bled out if you hadn't helped." He looked weary and confused.

A sound caused her to turn. The special agent had entered the hallway and stood staring at her. "I thought you were going to your residence." His voice was low and clipped.

"I was talking to Corporal Powers." She glanced back at the soldier. "I know this isn't the homecoming from the Middle East that you expected, with sick children and an injured wife. If it's any consolation, the girls are getting stronger, and I'm sure the doctors at Fort Rickman are doing everything they can for Mary Kate."

"When can I leave here?" he asked. "I need to go to the hospital to be with my wife, but the sergeant said he might have more questions."

"Maybe Special Agent Swain can help you."

Zach stepped forward, getting much too close to Ella. All she'd been able to smell since the storm was Georgia clay and dried blood. Now she inhaled the clean scent of sandalwood and a hint of lime.

She looked up, taking in his bulk, and then glanced down at her tattered blouse and soiled hands, realizing once again that she couldn't let appearance define her.

Ella wasn't who Quin had wanted her to be—that became evident over the course of their short marriage. The problem was, she wasn't sure who she was or what she wanted anymore. Quin had that effect on her. Or maybe it had started with her father, who was never satisfied with anything she did. How had she married a man who reminded her of her dad? A psychologist might say she was trying to prove her worth to both men, but she was tired of having to prove herself to anyone, even the special agent.

He touched her arm. She glanced down at a hand that would dwarf her own.

"Are you okay?" he asked, his voice brimming with concern.

Evidently, she had been lost in thought longer than she realized. "I'm fine. Thank you."

Turning abruptly on her heel, she followed the female police officer into her private residence and sighed as she closed the door behind her. Of course she wasn't fine.

She had been beaten up by an assailant who'd tried to shoot her.

The gun. Why hadn't she remembered the gun?

Ella hurried back into the hallway and stopped short in front of the treatment room. Zach moved to the door.

"Is something wrong?" he asked.

"The man...the assailant...he drew a weapon. The gun jammed. He kept trying to pull the trigger, over and over again."

The reality of her own brush with death overtook her. Tears burned her eyes. Her body trembled. Shock. She knew the signs, but couldn't help herself. She felt weak and sick and all alone.

Powerless to stop herself, she stepped toward the special agent with the wide shoulders and broad chest.

He opened his arms and pulled her into his embrace. "You're safe now."

Which was exactly how she felt. Then, all too quickly, she realized her mistake and pulled out of his hold.

"I'm sorry," she mumbled, embarrassed by her moment of weakness. Her cheeks burned as she retraced her steps and escaped into the kitchen.

Ella had hoped to find peace in Freemont, Georgia, but she'd found something else. She'd found a brutal attacker, a man who had tried to kill her. Why had he come into her clinic and what had he wanted to find?

Why had he opened his arms and pulled her into his embrace? Zach let out a stiff breath and mentally chastised himself for his emotional response to the doc. What was wrong with him tonight?

He stood staring after her as she closed the door at the end of the hallway, and willed himself to act like an investigator instead a guy taken in by a pretty face and big blue eyes. Inwardly, he shifted back to CID mode before he stepped into the treatment room where Corporal Powers waited.

After introducing himself, Zach inquired about the corporal's unit and why he had followed his wife and daughters to the clinic.

"I didn't follow them," the man insisted. "Mary Kate and the twins left the house when I was sleeping. The girls had been sick, and my wife mentioned calling the doctor."

"Dr. Jacobsen?"

The soldier nodded. "I figured they were here."

"So you came to find them."

"That's right."

"Tell me what happened when you arrived?"

"I already told the Freemont cop."

"But you need to tell me." Zach pulled out a notebook and held a pen over the tablet. He glanced at the young father and waited.

The sergeant clenched his hands. A muscle in his thick neck twitched.

Zach voiced his concern. "Does it make you angry to talk about what you saw, Corporal Powers?"

"I found my wife on the floor of this clinic. If it hadn't been for the doc, Mary Kate would have bled out. How would that make you feel?"

"Worried about my wife's condition."

"I was also worried about my girls. I thought they'd been killed. I was frantic."

"And angry?" Zach added. "Perhaps at your wife for leaving you and taking the children?"

The corporal shook his head. "I was angry that my wife was hurt, and fearful for my daughters. When I found them unharmed and sound asleep, I…I lost it." Hugh pulled in a ragged breath and rubbed his neck.

"You and your wife married when?"

"Five years ago. Soon after the girls were born. Mary

Kate was living in the Savannah area. I was stationed at Fort Stewart."

"She was pregnant when you met?"

"That's correct."

"Did you adopt the girls?" Zach asked.

"I'm their father." Anger flashed in his eyes. "Yes, I adopted them."

Other questions came to mind, like who was the biological father, but at that moment, Officer Abrams entered the room and nodded to Zach.

He posed one final question. "You're staying with your in-laws?"

"I am." The corporal nodded. "But right now, I want to go to the hospital and be with my wife."

"Looks like the Freemont police need to ask you some more questions." Zach handed the soldier his card. "Contact me if you remember anything else."

He handed a second card to Abrams. "I'll be in touch."

"You're taking the doc to the Freemont Hospital?"

"Roger that."

Zach returned to the office and studied the bloodstains on the floor. From the position of the blood spatter, he guessed Mary Kate had probably awakened, heard a noise and stumbled into the room, where the intruder had attacked her physically and then shot her with his weapon. Yet the doctor hadn't mentioned hearing gunfire.

He walked to where Taylor was lifting prints off the doctor's desk. "I was at Fort Rickman when the storm hit tonight. We had a lot of lightning and thunder. Was it the same around here?"

The young cop nodded. "Sounded like explosive blasts, one after another. Don't know when I've heard such deafening claps of thunder."

"Loud enough to muffle a gunshot?" Zach asked.

Taylor hesitated for a moment and then nodded. "As

loud as Mother Nature was tonight, anything could have been masked by the storm."

"Yet the doctor heard a scream."

"Which could have come between the lightning strikes. I don't think that's a problem, if you're wondering about what the doc remembers. Sergeant Abrams said she's got a bit of amnesia on top of shock. Her memory might return with time."

Zach peered down at the top of the desk. "Have you found any good prints?"

"A few partials. Whether we'll be able to identify anyone from them is the question. They're probably Dr. Jacobsen's or the nurse who works for her. I told you that we took the doc's prints earlier. We'll get the nurse's tomorrow. Won't take long before we know if we've got a match. I'm sure Sergeant Abrams will keep you informed."

"He's got my number."

An engraved invitation embossed with a caduceus logo and printed on heavy ecru card stock caught Zach's attention. He leaned closer, not wanting to touch anything on the desk until Taylor had finished his work.

"Cordially invited… Medical Symposium… Atlanta…" The event was scheduled for the upcoming Friday.

Zach rubbed his jaw. Somehow he couldn't see the rural doc fitting in at what appeared, from the fancy invitation, to be a rather highbrow event. Although maybe there was more to Ella Jacobsen than he realized.

The sound of footsteps caused him to look up as she entered the office. She was wearing gray slacks and a matching rust-colored sweater set. From the damp hair that curled around her face, he guessed she had taken time to shower.

As she stepped closer, he inhaled a fresh floral scent that contrasted sharply with the stale air in the clinic. A roomful of law enforcement types working extended shifts late into the night didn't do much for air quality.

"I appreciate you driving me to the hospital." Her apologetic smile looked more like a grimace. "I doubt there's anything wrong with me other than some scrapes and bruises, yet I always encourage my patients to be examined after any significant injury. I wouldn't be much of a doctor if I didn't practice what I preached."

"Going to the hospital is a good decision."

She glanced at Officer Taylor. "I usually don't leave my desk in such disarray." She tugged a strand of hair behind her ear. "I saw the man standing over it. Maybe he went through my papers."

Taylor pointed to an open cabinet. "Looks like he was going through your patient files, too, ma'am."

"I can't imagine why."

"Have you treated anyone recently that might not want their diagnosis revealed?" Zach asked. "Most folks don't want their medical information to end up in the wrong hands."

"I deal mainly with Amish children. I can't think of anything significant that my patients or their families would want to keep secret."

"What about the twins' condition? Is there any reason for that not to get out?"

Dr. Jacobsen shook her head. "Not that I know of."

"Maybe we'll find a match with one of the prints," Taylor said.

"Are you going to talk to my nurse in the morning?" she asked.

"Yes, ma'am. I'll get her prints then."

Zach pointed to the door. "If you're ready?"

She took a step forward and then hesitated. "I need to tell someone to turn off the lights and lock up when they leave."

The concern for her clinic was understandable. "I'll talk to Sergeant Abrams," Zach said. "Wait here and I'll be back in a minute."

He hurried to the treatment room where Corporal Powers stood with his back to the wall and his arms crossed over his chest. Antagonism was clearly written on his face. Abrams saw Zach and stepped into the hallway.

"I'm taking the doctor to the ER in town," Zach explained. "She's worried about her clinic and asked that the lights be turned off and the doors locked when you leave."

Abrams nodded. "We'll be here until the crime scene folks are finished. Could take most of the night, but tell her I'll make sure we leave the place secure."

"Hopefully, we'll be back before then, but knowing how slow emergency rooms can be, it might be hours before she's seen."

Abrams smiled knowingly. "Our local hospital isn't known for speed, so you're probably right. I'll contact you if we learn anything."

Pointing toward the treatment room, he added, "Corporal Powers is anxious about his wife. He plans to stay at the hospital on post. I imagine someone from your office will question him more thoroughly."

"I'll contact the CID," Zach assured the cop. "One of our people will visit Powers at the hospital. We'll contact his unit and ensure he's getting some support from their end. I'll check on his daughters and in-laws after the doc is treated. He's not a flight risk, and we know where to find him."

"I'll tell him to expect someone at the hospital."

Zach returned to the office, where the doc stood, her eyes wide as she looked around her, no doubt, once-tidy space. What had the assailant wanted? Two women were injured, one seriously, and medical files had been accessed.

In spite of what Abrams had suggested, the guy hadn't broken in looking for drugs. He wanted information or else to do harm. Maybe both. If only the Freemont police would uncover evidence they could use to track down the assailant. Until then the doctor needed to be careful and on guard, lest the guy return to do more damage.

Zach would keep watch, too. He didn't want anything else to happen to the doc.

THREE

If she made her patients wait this long she wouldn't have any. Ella sat in the exam room and hugged her arms around her chest, grateful that Zach hadn't deserted her. His frustration with medical personnel was evident by his frequent sighs and the pointed questions he asked the nurse concerning the lab results and CT scan. Yet he'd tried to buoy Ella's spirits and never complained about his own discomfort.

Of course, the nurse didn't have any way to speed up the lab technologists handling her specimens nor the CT techs, who had probably already given the results to the doctor. But Ella was beginning to feel as frustrated as Zach. Considering the number of patients in the waiting room when they'd arrived at the hospital hours ago, and the number of people who passed by in the hallway, if she received her test and lab results by lunchtime she would consider herself fortunate.

Not the way to run a hospital. Quin would have been equally as annoyed as the special agent, although her husband wouldn't have hung around while she was being treated. He would have mumbled some excuse about needing to get to his research, and left her to find her own transportation home.

Ella shook her head at the memory of what their life

together had been like, and then let out a lungful of air, mentally refusing to dwell on the past.

A tap sounded at the door.

She sat up straighter and raked her hand through her hair, not sure who to expect. "Come in."

The door opened, and Zach stepped into the exam room, carrying a white paper bag. "Two coffees from the cafeteria, one with cream and sugar, and two breakfast sandwiches. Egg and sausage sound okay?"

"Sounds delicious. How did you know I needed food?"

"Just a hunch." He glanced at the clock on the wall and then handed her a coffee and sandwich. "Patients could starve to death while they're waiting in the ER."

"I'll remember that in case I'm ever a hospital administrator." She accepted the food he offered.

"You'd be a good one, for sure."

She was taken aback by his comment. He was probably just being nice and making idle chitchat, but she was so accustomed to Quin's negativity that she hadn't expected anything as affirming and supportive. For some reason, she suddenly wanted to cry.

She blinked back the tears that stung her eyes, feeling totally foolish as she removed the plastic lid and took a sip of the hot brew. "Coffee was just what I needed."

Hopefully, he hadn't realized the emotional turmoil that had taken her by surprise. She blamed it on fatigue and her recent brush with death. If only her memory would return, so she could grasp exactly what had happened.

"I thought you'd stepped outside to make a phone call," she said as she unwrapped the sandwich.

"Actually, a number of calls. The first was to CID headquarters and the second to Corporal Powers's unit to ensure they knew what had happened."

"And did they?"

"He called them on his way to the hospital."

"Did you learn anything about Mary Kate's condition?"

"That was my third and final call. She remains critical and in ICU, but her husband is there, and so is her father."

"Maybe they'll offer each other support."

Ella and Zach ate the sandwiches, and by the time they'd finished their coffees, another tap sounded at the door.

"I'll wait in the hallway." Zach left the room as the doctor entered.

"Did I scare him off?" the physician asked.

Ella appreciated Zach's thoughtfulness in leaving so she could talk to the clinician, who seemed oblivious to the importance of patient privacy.

"I'm sure my labs were in normal range," she said, to get the doctor back on track. "But what about the CT scan?"

"You have a slight concussion, so I want you to take it easy for the next twenty-four to forty-eight hours. Continue to ice that lump on your head. You might have headaches for a day or so. Expect muscle soreness, especially where you were kicked. Ibuprofen will help or I can prescribe something stronger."

She held up her hand. "That won't be necessary."

"I don't know if you're a churchgoing woman, but I believe in God's benevolence. He was watching over you last night."

His comment took her aback. She'd never had much of a relationship with God in her youth and had stopped asking for His help when her marriage had fallen apart.

"You were fortunate not to have broken ribs," the ER doc continued. "Or something worse. If anything changes, don't hesitate to come back. I doubt you'll have to wait as long next time."

"I'm hoping there won't be a next time."

"We're short staffed right now, Dr. Jacobsen." He

tapped her file. "If you are looking for some weekend or evening work, I'm sure the personnel office would be happy to accept your application for employment."

She smiled at the job offer. "Thanks, but my patients keep me busy."

"I'm sure. We don't see many Amish at the hospital. Every once in a while we'll set a broken bone or tend to some farm injury. As you probably know, the plain folk usually tend to their own medical needs. I know they probably appreciate having you in their area."

"Some do. Some don't."

He nodded. "That's always the way. I wish you the best with your clinic. Let us know if we can be of help."

Ella appreciated his comments almost as much as she was grateful for the clean bill of health. She found Zach in the hallway, and after receiving her treatment notes from the nurse, hurried with him to his car.

He opened the door to the passenger side and held her arm as she settled in the seat. She wasn't used to such attention, but wouldn't do anything to dampen his enthusiasm or good manners.

"I'm glad you're okay," he said.

"Just a little tired, which I'm sure you are, as well. Thank you again."

"No problem." He was silent until they turned onto the main road leading to the Amish community. "I need to know a bit more about Mary Kate, if you feel up to talking."

"I don't know much about her family. She mentioned an older brother in Atlanta."

"Any family history of violence?" Zach asked.

Ella looked down at her hands folded in her lap and weighed what she should tell the special agent. She needed to be truthful, but she also worried about the young family, who seemed to have so many problems.

"Her husband was recently diagnosed with PTSD."

Zach kept his eyes on the road, but pursed his lips before he asked, "Do you know if he's had any volatile incidents?"

"She mentioned a few problems, but nothing about any outbursts on his part. Still, she might have glossed over the severity of their situation."

"One of the CID agents from post plans to question him later today."

"Is he a suspect?"

Zach shook his head. "Not at this point."

"You're sure? Because if you do suspect him, then I'd be worried about the twins' safety."

"After I drop you off, Doc, I plan to pay the grandparents a visit."

"We'll go together. Their house is on the way."

"Didn't the ER doctor prescribe rest?"

"A house call won't tax me unduly. Plus it will ease my mind to know the girls are all right."

"We'll make a short visit. Then you're going straight home."

"Aye aye, sir."

He laughed. "You're mixing branches of the service."

"Whatever works." She smiled. "But do me a favor. My first name's Ella."

"And I'm Zach."

She pointed to the upcoming intersection. "Turn right. Then make another right at the four-way."

She stole a glance at his sturdy shoulders and strong hands. Quin had been a small man. Zach was the exact opposite. He was all brawn and muscle, with deep-set eyes that continued to glance at her.

The strange ripple of interest she felt surprised her. Her marriage had been a failure. She wouldn't try again with any man. Her clinic and her work provided everything she needed. And more.

"There's the house. On the left." She pointed to the two-story colonial with a circular driveway.

"I don't want you to overdo it," Zach cautioned again.

"I'm okay. Really. Ensuring the twins' condition has improved will be better than any meds the doctor at the hospital could have prescribed."

After Zach parked, Ella stepped from the car. Together, they walked to the front door, and he rang the bell.

Lucy Landers, the twins' grandmother, cracked open the door. Her hair was pulled into a bun, and she wore a white apron over a calico dress. "Yes?"

"Mrs. Landers, I'm Dr. Jacobsen from the Children's Care Clinic. I've been treating the twins and wanted to ensure they were feeling better."

"Oh, forgive me, Dr. Jacobsen. I didn't recognize you." She opened the door wide. "Come in, please."

Ella introduced Zach. "Special Agent Swain is from Fort Rickman. He's investigating what happened at my clinic."

The older woman's eyes filled with tears. "My husband has been at the hospital all night. The doctors told him the next twenty-four hours are so important."

Ella reached for her hand. "The medical personnel know what they're doing."

Mrs. Landers sniffed. "I hope you're right."

Ella glanced around the living room with its simple furnishings, and peered into the hallway. "What about the girls?"

"They're still sleeping."

"Did either child run a temperature in the night?" she asked.

The woman shook her head. "I checked them often. They stayed cool."

"May I see them, Mrs. Landers?"

"Of course." She motioned for Ella and Zach to follow her, and stopped at the threshold of a small bedroom where the twins lay sleeping.

Ella quietly approached the double bed and touched each child's forehead, relieved that both girls felt cool and afebrile. One of the twins blinked her eyes open.

"Hi, Stacey." Ella smiled down at her. "How are you feeling?"

"Fine."

"Does your tummy hurt anymore?"

The little girl shook her head. "I'm hungry."

Ella glanced at the grandmother. "Seems Stacey is ready for breakfast."

"I'm so glad." The woman held out her hand. "Come on, sugar. Let's go into the kitchen. I'll fix you a soft-boiled egg on toast. Won't that taste good?"

The child looked at her sister. "What about Shelly?"

"She'll wake up soon, sugar. When she does, I'll make her an egg, too."

Ella checked the second twin, who stirred and then snuggled down even deeper into the bedding.

"Thanks for bringing me here," Ella whispered to Zach as they left the room. "I'm relieved knowing the girls are better."

"Can I fix something for you folks?" Lucy asked from the kitchen. "How 'bout some coffee?"

"I need to get back to the clinic," Ella said. "If anything changes, call me there."

The front door opened and the twins' grandfather entered the house. Heavyset and in his late fifties, Mr. Landers wore a plaid shirt and dark slacks.

"Are the girls sick again?" he asked in lieu of a greeting.

"No, sir." Ella shook her head. "Both of them seem better. Stacey's in the kitchen waiting for your wife to fix her something to eat. Shelly's sleeping, but her fever has broken. I expect both girls to be back to normal by tomorrow morning."

She introduced Zach.

"You're from the fort?" the older man asked.

"That's right, sir. I'm with the Criminal Investigation Division. We're looking into your daughter's attack. Mrs. Landers said you were with her at the hospital on post. How's her condition?"

"The doctor said she's critical and wouldn't let me stay with her long."

"That's standard policy for patients in intensive care," Ella tried to explain.

He nodded. "Hugh and I took turns. He's having a hard time, and I'm worried about him."

"Grandpa!" Stacey ran from the kitchen and into his open arms.

"How's my Sassafras?"

"I'm not your Sassafras, Grandpa. I'm your Sweet Tea."

His eyes widened. "Then you're not Shelly?"

The little girl giggled. "Shelly's a sleepyhead. Grandma said she'd wake up soon."

"You're feeling better, honey?"

The child nodded. "And hungry. Grandma wants to know if you'll eat some eggs."

"Tell Grandma I'm hungry enough to eat a bear."

The girl laughed and raced back to the kitchen. "Grandpa wants bear with his eggs."

The older man's eyes clouded. "Don't know what we'd do without those girls."

"Sir, does anyone come to mind who might want to harm your daughter?" Zach asked.

He hesitated. "Hard to say."

"So there is someone?"

Mr. Landers nodded. "Levi Miller."

"Has he caused problems, sir?"

"Not problems, but he's passed by a number of times in the last couple months."

"I'm sure many Amish farmers and their families drive their buggies in front of your house," Ella said. "You live on one of the main roads in this area."

"But Levi is different."

"How so, sir?" Zach asked.

"He always had his eye on Mary Kate."

"Levi has a wife," Ella insisted. "They're expecting a child."

Landers snarled. "That doesn't make a bit of difference to some men. If I see him hanging around again, I'll give him a piece of my mind."

"Might be wise to notify the police, sir, if you have a grievance against Mr. Miller," Zach cautioned.

The older man bristled. "I can take care of my family and don't need the cops."

"Sir, your daughter is in ICU. Someone shot her. I beg to differ. You do need law enforcement." Zach handed the man his card. "If you see Levi around here, call me. I'll question him."

"I'm not sure you can help." Mr. Landers excused himself and headed for the kitchen. "You folks can let yourselves out."

When they'd stepped outside, Zach turned to Ella. "At some point, I'll need to talk to Levi Miller."

"Let me know when, and I'll go with you. Levi's wife is a patient of mine." Ella headed for the car and thanked Zach as he held the door for her, before he rounded the vehicle and slipped behind the wheel.

"Mr. Landers isn't a very welcoming man," he said as he turned the car onto the road.

"He's worried and not thinking rationally."

"I'm sure that's the case," Zach agreed, "although there might be some truth to what he told us."

Ella didn't want to see Levi pulled into the investigation. He was a good man and a helpful neighbor. Again, she thought of how life had changed since the attack.

Staring out the window, she took in the rolling hills and farmland that she loved. In the distance, she could see a number of Amish homes. Their way of life had attracted her after Quin's death, when she didn't know where to go or to whom to turn. She'd found comfort here and a sense of welcome from some of the families.

But all that had changed when the intruder broke in last night. Could he have been stalking Mary Kate? If so, Ella refused to believe that Levi was the assailant. He was a man of peace with a sweet wife and a baby on the way.

Zach parked in her driveway and walked her to the front door of the clinic. She pulled the key from her purse, stuck it in the lock and turned the knob.

Glancing into the waiting room, she gasped. Her heart skittered in her chest and the fear she had felt last night returned full force.

"What's wrong?" Zach asked, dropping his hand protectively on her shoulder.

"The attacker," she whispered, unable to control the tremble in her voice. "He returned. This time, he destroyed my clinic."

FOUR

Zach grabbed Ella's arm and stopped her from entering the clinic. "Wait in the car. You'll be safer there. I want to check inside to make sure no one's lying in wait."

Her eyes widened. "You think the attacker from last night came back?"

"He wanted something he didn't find. Any idea what that could be?"

She shook her head. "I don't know. I...I thought he was after Mary Kate."

"Which might be the case. What about the children's medical records? Could there be something in their charts that he doesn't want revealed?"

"Maybe."

Zach stared at Ella for a long moment and then pointed to the car. "Stay in my vehicle and keep the doors locked while I search the clinic."

Thankfully, she complied with his instructions and hurried there. She slipped into the passenger seat, hit the lock button and nodded to him when she was securely inside.

Zach pulled out his phone and called Sergeant Abrams. "I'm at the Children's Care Clinic. Looks like the perpetrator from last night came back. I'm going in to do a search. The doc is outside in my car. I'd appreciate a couple of your people to process the scene. We might find a print that matches something from last night."

Disconnecting, he tugged back his jacket and slipped his SIG Sauer from its holster. He doubted the perp was still on-site, yet he didn't want to go in unprepared. The guy wanted something, or perhaps he'd left something behind and returned to retrieve whatever he'd lost.

Cautiously, Zach entered the clinic, his eyes scanning the room, left to right. He hugged the wall and stepped through the waiting area. The door to the office hung open. Zach stared through the doorway, searching for anything amiss.

The perp had been thorough. The drawers of the doctor's desk hung open, and the contents lay scattered on the floor. Manila folders from the file cabinet were strewn helter-skelter about the room.

Had he been hunting for a certain patient's records? If so, who and why?

Zach checked the closets, where someone could be hiding. The medication cabinet was locked. From all appearances, drugs hadn't been the reason for the break-in.

After moving into the hallway, Zach searched the two treatment rooms, then headed to the door that opened into Ella's residence.

He entered the kitchen, a warm and welcoming room with a round table positioned in front of a bay window. A yellow print tablecloth matched the valances that hung at the windows, and a bouquet of fall flowers adorned the middle of the table.

Zach remembered his home when his mother was still alive. She'd loved flowers and always had them in the house.

They bring God's beautiful nature indoors, he recalled her saying as she'd arranged a bouquet in a crystal vase that had been passed down from her mother. The memory made him pause and stare at the mums on the doc's table. His mother had been a woman of faith, but God didn't play favorites. Or so it seemed.

Shaking off those thoughts, he moved quickly through the living room, then checked the master bedroom with an attached bath and the guest room with its own bath. A third room served as an office. Unlike the clinic, this one had pictures of children on the wall. Zach stepped closer.

A few of the girls wore long dresses, and some boys had dark trousers and hats that covered their bobbed hair. Amish children. From what he knew of the sect, they didn't like photographs. Evidently the doc had gotten special permission to snap the shots.

Diplomas from a number of universities hung near the pictures, along with a picture of Ella and a slender man of medium height with deep-set eyes. He was frowning, as if the photographer had surprised him when he didn't want his photo taken.

Ella stood awkwardly at his side, her hand reaching for his. Had the stoic husband rejected his wife's attempt at closeness, or was that merely Zach's imagination adding a dramatic spin to the reality of what Ella's life had been?

He liked to think he could read people, but the doc was a closed book. Her husband appeared to be equally hard to read.

Turning from the photos, Zach backtracked through the clinic and hurried outside to where Ella waited in his car.

"Did you find anything?" She opened the door as he neared.

"Nothing except a lot of chaos in your office. The treatment area and your residence seem untouched, but the guy was looking for something. Patient records are scattered on the floor. Any ideas?"

"None at all. You tell me what someone might want."

"Information. He attacked Mary Kate. Perhaps he followed her to your clinic, then cut the electricity so he could enter in the dark. He attacks her, probably thought he had killed her, which may have been his goal."

Ella's hand rose to her throat. "I can't imagine anyone wanting to do her harm."

"What information could he be searching for in your patient files? Tell me about the girls' condition."

She shrugged. "Childhood enzyme deficiency is a newly emerging condition. There's a symposium this coming Friday in Atlanta that will focus on a number of conditions, including CED, followed by a charity dinner that will celebrate the research center's success. The proceeds raised will help Amish families with their medical bills and also fund the clinic to ensure the research continues."

"The research center is where your husband worked?"

"That's right. The Harrisburg Genetic Research Center." She pointed to her clinic. "Now if you don't mind, I need to go inside and assess the damage."

Zach held up his hand. "Not yet. The local authorities have to process the crime scene first. You wouldn't want to contaminate the evidence."

"Contamination is something found on a petri dish," she groused.

He tried not to smile, knowing she didn't think waiting on the porch was humorous. Nor did he, but her nose wiggled sometimes when she was upset, which he found amusing, if not charming.

"Does anyone else have a key to your office?"

"Just my nurse and nurse-receptionist, but I trust them completely. I'm more inclined to think someone didn't secure the doors last night. Who was the last one here?"

"We'll ask the officers when they arrive. Sergeant Abrams is on the way."

Ella rubbed her forehead. "Everything still seems so foggy about the attack. I lost consciousness briefly. Short-term memory loss sometimes follows, which seems to be the case."

"Have you remembered anything else?"

She shook her head. "Only my surprise in finding someone standing by my desk. He raised the light he was carrying, and I was caught in its glare. I couldn't see his face. Then…"

Zach saw the anguish in her eyes.

"I…I remember his kicks. The pain. I couldn't breathe."

"You fought back."

"Did I?"

Zach reached for her hand. "Look at your nails and the scratches on your skin."

She glanced down at her broken fingernails and scraped knuckles.

"Does that surprise you?" he asked.

"A little, but it makes me glad. Quin…" She hesitated before adding, "My husband claimed I never stood up for myself."

"Maybe you didn't need to assert yourself when he was around."

"You mean because Quin kept me safe?"

Zach nodded. "That sounds logical to me."

"From what I've seen of you, Special Agent Swain, you are a protector. My husband? Not so much."

Her comment about being a protector gave him pause. He hadn't been able to protect his mother, and while that was long ago and he'd been a young boy, the memory troubled him still.

"You're a doctor," he said, hoping to deflect the conversation away from himself. "You save lives. That's a big responsibility."

"I like children. Being a pediatrician seemed like a good fit, but you're giving me more credit than I deserve."

Before Zach could reply, a patrol car raced along Amish

Road and turned into the clinic drive. Sergeant Abrams stepped from the car and nodded as he approached.

"Doctor." He glanced at Zach. "Long time no see, Special Agent Swain."

"Sorry to call you out again." Zach extended his hand. In short, clipped sentences he explained the chain of events that had them hanging out on the porch of her clinic.

"I'd like to go inside as soon as possible to assess any damage that may have occurred," Ella said.

"Yes, ma'am. Just as soon as we take some photos and make a sketch of what we find."

"We?" She glanced into his car, then raised her gaze as another police sedan approached the clinic and turned into the parking lot.

"Officer Taylor," Abrams said by way of an introduction as the driver came forward.

"Sir." The younger cop nodded respectfully before shaking Ella's and Zach's hands.

"We met last night," Zach said with a smile.

"You brought your camera?" the sergeant asked.

"Yes, sir. I'll take pictures inside. Shouldn't be too long."

"I don't see why I can't enter my own clinic," Ella complained.

"Let us get the photos first. Then I'll want to talk to you," Abrams explained.

"More questions?"

"Yes, ma'am."

The two officers entered the clinic. Ella turned to Zach. "You don't have to babysit me."

He didn't need to hear the frustration in her voice or see the firm set of her jaw to know the doc was upset. "This is all SOP—standard operating procedure—with law enforcement. It's not personal, Ella."

"Remind me to tell you the same thing when your office is trashed."

Perhaps he needed to be more considerate. Getting her mind on something other than her clinic might help.

Zach pointed to the small house on the property next door. "Tell me about your neighbor."

Ella followed his gaze. "Levi Miller and his wife, Sarah, are a nice young couple. They're expecting their first child. Sarah is a patient."

"You deliver babies, too?"

"I can. The Amish hesitate going to large medical facilities and prefer to have Amish midwives or other local medical personnel assist with their deliveries."

"You've been here five months, and it seems you have a good number of patients from the charts strewn about the office."

"I had trouble at first. After the first couple of families sought my help when their children were sick, word spread. Cash can be a problem for the Amish. Sometimes I'm paid in produce or baked goods, sometimes homemade sausage and milk and cheese."

"That hardly covers your mortgage."

"No, but I get by."

"What'd you do before this?" Zach asked.

"You mean in Pennsylvania?"

He nodded. "You talked about your husband, but you haven't mentioned what you did."

"Quin worked for a research clinic that was headquartered in Harrisburg, as I probably told you last night." She raked her hand through her hair. "I'm still fuzzy on a lot of things."

"I thought the Amish were in Lancaster County."

"That's the largest community, but Amish live near Carlisle, as well. Besides, a well-known clinic handles the area around the towns of Intercourse and Bird-in-Hand. Quin's group covered some of the other areas."

"And you?" Zach asked.

"I had a pediatric clinic in Carlisle."

"Where the Army War College is located."

"You've been there?" she asked.

"A few years back. Carlisle seemed like a nice place. Dickinson College is located there."

"That's right."

"What made you move South?" he asked.

She tilted her head and shrugged. "I needed a change. I would always be Quin Jacobsen's widow if I stayed there. I wanted to make my own way." She smiled weakly. "That sounds self-serving, but I don't mean it in that way. Quin was a larger-than-life type of guy, speaking academically. Sometimes I felt dwarfed by his presence."

From the short time Zach had known Ella, she seemed down-to-earth and committed to her patients. Thinking of the picture he'd seen of her in the office, he could understand what she was saying.

She rubbed her hands together and glanced at her clinic. "What's taking so long?"

"I'll check." Zach hurried inside and found Abrams. "The doc wants to assess the damage. Have you gotten all the photos you need?"

"Almost. Taylor needs to take a couple of her desk and then we'll be finished."

"What about fingerprints?"

"We lifted a few from the file cabinet and the folders strewn over the floor. Two or three look promising. I'll run them when I get back to headquarters."

"You'll let me know?"

"As soon as I hear anything."

As Taylor snapped shots of the desk, Zach stepped closer. He leaned over the engraved invitation he'd seen the night before.

Abrams glanced over his shoulder. "From the looks of

that, the event appears to be a snazzy gathering. The doc seems more like a country girl."

"I'm sure she would fit in no matter the environment."

"You're probably right." The older officer looked around the clinic. "Looks like we've got what we need for now. Tell the doc she can come inside."

When Zach opened the door, he was surprised to see a young man standing on the porch with her.

Ella introduced him as he neared. "Special Agent Swain, this is my neighbor, Levi Miller."

The neighbor was dressed in the typical dark slacks held up with suspenders. A wide-brimmed hat sat atop his blond hair, and he wore a cotton shirt probably sewn by his wife.

"You live in the next house?" Zach pointed to the small one-story home.

"*Yah*. My wife and I live there."

"Did you hear anything last night, Mr. Miller?"

"I heard the storm."

"Did you hear sirens or see the police here?"

The man's face clouded. "My wife glanced from the window. She was worried about Dr. Jacobsen."

"But you didn't check on her last night," Zach pressed.

"That's why I came today." The Amish man turned to Ella. "You are all right?"

"Someone broke into the clinic. He shot Mary Kate Powers."

Levi's face blanched. "She was hurt?"

Ella touched the Amish man's arm. "Quite seriously, I'm afraid. She's at the hospital on post and is in critical condition."

"May *Gott's* will be done."

Zach didn't understand the comment. "You know Mary Kate?"

"Her parents have a home not far from here. We knew each other as children."

Zach wondered if that friendship had continued into adulthood.

"What about the twins?" Levi asked. The concern in his voice was clearly obvious.

"They're fine," Ella assured him. "Thankfully, they were asleep in the treatment room, and the attacker left through the front door after accosting their mother."

Levi let out a ragged breath. "I am relieved."

"You know the twins?" Zach asked.

The Amish man steeled his gaze. "Twins are easy to recognize, Special Agent Swain. They have been getting treatments at the Children's Care Clinic for some months now. I have a farm and work outside. Of course I have seen them."

"What would you call your relationship with their mother?" Zach remembered the grandfather's words about the Amish man who seemed much too attentive to his daughter.

"There is no relationship."

"You haven't tried to reconnect with Mary Kate?" Zach asked.

"A married man has eyes only for his wife." He looked at Ella. "If you need my help, let me know."

"Thank you, Levi."

With a nod, he turned and walked back to his property.

Zach watched him enter his house. "There's something Levi's not telling us."

Ella lowered her gaze, as if she, too, had something to hide.

Zach stared down at her. "Is there something about Levi that I need to know?"

"Of course not." After an abrupt about-face, Ella pushed open the door to her clinic and stepped inside.

Zach glanced back at the Miller farm. A cold wind whipped across the expansive pasture area and along the road, picking up dust and blowing it in the air.

What was the truth about this Amish community and the doctor who had left her practice in Pennsylvania to move South? Was she being less than forthright? If so, why?

All her work had seemingly been for naught. Standing at the entrance to her clinic, Ella was overcome with despair. She had tried to create an environment where Amish children, used to the simple basics in their own homes, could be comfortable even when they were sick and upset. Surrounded by medical instrumentation and equipment, they could easily become wide-eyed and fearful, which only made their parents more on edge. The adults were often torn between their concern for their sick children and their own hesitation to trust the new doctor.

As she gazed at the disarray, Ella wondered what they would think if they saw the place in such a state of chaos. Her hard work up to this point and her dreams of what the clinic could be in the future had been all but dashed by the hand of a madman.

"Who would do this?" she asked, struggling to articulate even that brief question. Wrapping her arms around her chest, she glanced at the officers, who had stopped processing the crime scene and were staring at her.

Did they think she was becoming hysterical?

Zach entered the clinic behind her and touched her arm. Was he offering comfort or was he, too, afraid she might be ready for a breakdown?

"Who was the last person in here last night?" Ella demanded, feeling a swell of anger. She stared at Abrams. "Did you lock the door? Did you secure my clinic or did you leave the door open and vulnerable to the madman, who returned to find what he'd wanted the first time?"

They continued to look at her as if she were crazed, and perhaps she was—crazed with frustration at all that had happened.

Abrams stepped forward. "I asked one of my officers to make sure your clinic was secure. I trust he did as I directed."

Officer Taylor moved closer. "The assailant could have had a key. You know he cut your power, ma'am. It wasn't the storm that caused your outage. Someone tampered with your wiring. We got it working last night, and I checked your generator. The spark plug had been unscrewed. No wonder it wouldn't engage."

"So someone was prowling around here before the storm?" She shivered at the thought of the assailant stalking her and her clinic.

"Seems that way. Is there anyone who'd want to do you harm?"

"No, not that I know of." She glanced at Zach, hoping he would offer some other reason for the attack.

"The young mother, Mary Kate Powers, might have some bearing on the case," he volunteered. "Her husband recently returned from the Middle East. Her father is concerned about the Amish man who lives next door."

"You mean Levi Miller?" Abrams asked.

"Levi wouldn't have done anything to harm Mary Kate," Ella was quick to point out.

"Why do you say that, ma'am?" the sergeant asked.

"He and Mary Kate knew each other in their youth. I believe they were close friends."

The cop looked puzzled. "Amish and English, as they call us, make for an unusual friendship."

"They were young, Sergeant Abrams. That hardly seems strange to me."

"Yes, ma'am, but Mary Kate would have gone to Freemont High," the sergeant said. "Levi Miller would have received his instruction at the Amish schoolhouse."

"They could still be friends even if they didn't go to school together," she insisted. "The Landerses live in this area. Amish children roam the fields and think nothing of walking great distances. They don't have the fear that keeps some of the town children from wandering far from their homes."

Ella looked at Zach and then back to the Freemont officer. "As you probably know, the Amish children work hard, but when their chores are finished they're free spirits. I can see Mary Kate getting to know Levi as a youngster."

"Yet her father seems to harbor a grudge against Levi," Zach interjected.

"Landers holds a grudge against a number of people in the local community," Abrams volunteered. "He's known as a grumpy old man."

"Are you saying his animosity toward Levi should be ignored?" Zach asked.

"Hardly." The sergeant shook his head. "We'll take everything into consideration, but I'm not going to falsely accuse anyone based on what a crusty old codger has to say."

As Zach and he continued to discuss the case, Ella rubbed her neck. Her head pounded and her body ached from the attack last night. Ibuprofen would help, but she didn't want medication, she wanted to breathe in fresh air and feel the sunshine on her face. A more holistic approach to healing.

"If you'll excuse me for a minute, I've got a patio out back," she said. "I just need some air."

Rubbing her temple, she hurried into her kitchen and out the back door. She had expected warm sunshine, but was instantly chilled by a stiff wind that blew from the west. Wrapping her arms around herself, she stared into the wooded area behind her house, seeing the fall colors and the branches swaying in the breeze. Overhead, geese honked, flying in a V formation. If only she could fly away from the chaos like them and find a peaceful spot to land that would calm her troubled spirit.

Movement caught her eye and she glanced again at the woods. What had she seen? An animal foraging in the underbrush?

Or…

Ella narrowed her gaze and took a step back as if subconsciously recognizing danger. Her heart lurched. She turned and ran for the protection of her house. Tripping, she fell on the steps.

A sound exploded in the quiet of the day.

A ceramic flowerpot shattered at her feet.

Another shot was fired and then another.

She screamed, stumbled up the porch stairs and reached for the door.

Zach was there, pulling her inside to safety. He shoved her to the floor and slammed the door. "Stay down."

"A man," she gasped, her pulse racing, a roar filling her ears. "In the woods. He—he had a rifle…"

Zach lifted the curtain ever so slightly and stared through the window.

The two policemen raced into the kitchen. "Gunfire?"

Zach pointed. "The doc saw a man at the edge of the forest."

"A dirt road runs parallel to the tree line." Sergeant Abrams motioned to the younger officer. "We'll head there from opposite directions."

Abrams radioed for more squad cars. "There's a shooter in the woods behind the Children's Care Clinic. We need to search the area and set up roadblocks. Someone needs to check the wooden bridge that's along that road, as well."

Zach locked the doors when the two officers had left, racing away in their squad cars. The sound of sirens filled the air as more Freemont police responded to the call.

Ella huddled against the wall in the corner, while Zach kept watch at the windows. The tension that lined his face spoke volumes about the danger, but she didn't need to look at him to know that the situation had escalated.

What she realized made her tremble with fear. Last night, the police were looking for an assailant who had broken into her clinic and attacked two women.

Today that assailant had become a killer.

And the person he wanted to kill was her.

FIVE

"We found spent rifle casings at the edge of the tree line," Sergeant Abrams said, holding up the evidence bag to Ella, when he and Officer Taylor returned to the clinic. Seeing the casings made her feel even less secure.

"Looks like thirty caliber." Zach stepped closer and studied the back of one of the rounds. "They're 30-30 to be exact."

Abrams nodded. "Someone was holed up for a period of time, judging from the way the underbrush was trampled down. Could have been the guy from last night. He hides in the woods and watches for the doc to return, only he can't see the parking lot in front of the clinic."

"So he didn't see squad cars parked there and didn't realize law enforcement was on-site," Zach mused.

"That's what I'm thinking." The sergeant scratched his chin. "If he didn't find what he wanted last night, he could have waited for the doctor to return."

"You're sure he was after me?" Ella rubbed her hands together, trying to dispel her nervousness.

"Seems that way, although we can't be sure," the cop said. "Folks who commit crimes aren't always the smartest people. He might have another reason to be lying in wait. We'll process the prints we took earlier and see if any are on the shell casings. We might find new prints that match what we lifted last night. That would mean the attacker came back. If not, we could be dealing with two independent crimes, although that doesn't seem likely." He looked at Zach. "Anything come to mind?"

"Never say never."

Abrams nodded. "That's exactly the way I feel."

The two Freemont officers headed for the door. "We'll increase patrols in this area and keep our eyes open in case the shooter returns, but we're finished here for now," Abrams said. "We'll stop by Mr. Miller's farm and talk to him. Join us, Special Agent Swain, if you have time."

Zach nodded. "I appreciate the offer, but I'll talk to Levi a bit later. If he happens to reveal anything of value, I'd like to be notified."

"Will do." Abrams turned to Ella. "Might be a good idea to install dead bolts and even an alarm system, Dr. Jacobsen. A watchdog would be a deterrent to crime, as well. Keep your cell charged and near you at all times. You might want to move to town until this case is solved."

"I'm staying here, Sergeant Abrams. My patients need to know where to find me. I wouldn't be much good to them if I was holed up in a hotel in town. Besides, I refuse to run scared."

"I wouldn't call that running, ma'am. I'd call it being prudent and safe."

The cop shook Zach's hand and nodded to her. "I'll be in touch, Dr. Jacobsen. Don't hesitate to call us if you think of anything that might have a bearing on this case."

"I'll be sure to do that."

The officers left the house yet again. Ella stood at the window and watched as they climbed into their patrol cars. Then, letting out a deep sigh, she turned her gaze to the Miller home.

Levi's wife, Sarah, was a sweet young woman, though somewhat reserved. Ella hoped that everything that had happened wouldn't upset her unduly or cause her more worry. The baby was due in three months. Hopefully, the birth would be uneventful, but the last thing Ella wanted was for the young wife to be distressed.

Zach stepped to her side and followed her gaze. "You're worried about Levi?"

"I'm more concerned about Sarah and their baby. They've requested genetic testing, but the results won't come back for some time."

"Do you suspect a problem?"

"There's no way to tell until I hear from the lab."

"Could the Miller baby have the same condition as the twins?"

Ella nodded. "It's a possibility."

Zach started to say something, but her office phone rang. She reached for the receiver.

"Children's Care Clinic. This is Dr. Jacobsen."

"It's Nancy Vaughn, Ella."

The director of the research center where Quin had worked.

"Is something wrong, Dr. Vaughn?"

"Actually, I'm calling to make sure you're all right. A reporter from the *Atlanta Journal-Constitution* asked for a statement about the medical symposium this Friday. He wanted to know if Dr. Jacobsen's widow would be attending. I haven't heard from you and thought there might be a problem."

"You don't need me there, Dr. Vaughn."

"Quin's death hit us hard, as you know, Ella. We were in the midst of gathering data and coming up with our final determination. Now that the studies have been completed, we want to recognize Quin."

"I hardly think that's necessary."

"Don't keep us from honoring one of our own, Ella."

"No, of course I wouldn't do that."

"Then it's settled. You'll come to Atlanta and be with us this Friday. Freemont is only two hours from the city. There's no reason to stay away."

Ella picked up the embossed invitation. "Perhaps I'll come for the symposium…"

"And the dinner following," the director insisted. "I want you there. It's a black-tie event, so that's a good excuse to get a new dress. I'll look forward to seeing you."

"I'm not sure."

"I won't take no for an answer."

Nancy Vaughn was like that.

Before the director could hang up, Ella quickly added, "Did you review Quin's data on the Amish Project? I've looked through most of his notes, but I can't find any discrepancies."

"Discrepancies? Why are you questioning his work?"

"I'm not, but something bothered him, as I told you when we last talked. He was concerned about the response of twin patients who were given the treatment."

"There were no problems, as I already told you."

"But—"

"No buts. We'll see you Friday."

The director disconnected before Ella could say anything else.

She sighed as she hung up the phone, and then looked up to see Zach staring at her.

"Is something wrong?" he asked.

She shook her head. "No, nothing's wrong. My husband's research center is discussing their findings on CED."

"The disease the twins have?"

Ella nodded. "I called the director when Mary Kate first brought the girls to the clinic."

"It sounded as if you were concerned about something your husband found."

"Quin was intense, especially when he was working toward a breakthrough. He became more and more upset about some results that he couldn't understand. He kept saying the Amish twins held the answer."

"You're not talking about Shelly and Stacey."

"No, there were other cases. Three sets of twins that hadn't responded the way he had hoped."

"You mentioned his notes on the Amish Project?"

"That's what the CED study was called. The director, Dr. Nancy Vaughn, never wanted work taken home. There's always a worry that some other clinic will get access to the data and use it as their own."

"Stealing data for scientific gain or for financial compensation?" he asked.

"Probably both, although I don't think Quin ever worried about his work being stolen. He was more concerned about why the treatment he had developed wasn't effective."

"The director couldn't offer any answers?" Zach pressed.

"She has a lot on her mind and seemed surprised the last time we talked about Quin taking his notes home. I assured her he was careful to keep his files secure."

"You've gone through his notes?"

"And found nothing."

"Does that seem strange to you?"

Ella weighed her words. She didn't want the special agent to jump to the wrong conclusions. "Quin's entire focus was on his work, especially close to his death."

Zach stared at her. "Does that mean he turned his focus away from you?"

It wasn't a question she expected. "I didn't say that."

"But it's what you didn't say."

She shook her head, suddenly flustered. "You're reading more into my statement."

"Am I?"

She dropped the invitation onto her desk and bent to pick up some of the scattered papers.

"I'm sorry if I upset you, Ella."

"It's not you." She let out a deep breath. "It's everything that's happened."

"You'll feel better once the clinic is back in order. I'll help you."

"I don't need help," she insisted, although she did. But right now she was so confused and worried. Would her life ever get back to the way it had been?

"Perhaps you don't, but I'm not leaving you alone with so much to do," Zach insisted.

"You sound as strong-willed as my husband."

Instantly, she regretted her remark. Zach wasn't strong-willed, and he wasn't anything like her husband. When she looked at Zach, she saw compassion and understanding in his gaze.

At least she thought she did.

Or was she as wrong about Zach as she had been about Quin?

Zach encouraged Ella to sit and direct him as he cleaned up the clinic, but evidently, she didn't trust him to get it right, because she insisted on doing everything herself. At least she let him install the dead bolts she had bought some weeks earlier but hadn't taken out of the shopping bag.

She had a toolbox filled with the basics, one that might have belonged to her husband. Although if the tools had been his, then Quin Jacobsen hadn't been much of a handyman. Still, Zach found what he needed and soon had the dead bolts installed.

He checked her windows, relieved to find double-paned glass and substantial locks that would be hard to pry open.

"Sergeant Abrams mentioned a security alarm," Zach reminded Ella, after securing the doors and checking the windows. "Even the most basic, easy-to-install wireless system, would be an excellent safeguard."

She cocked her head and frowned. "And if the alarm goes off, who comes to my rescue?"

"The alarm service calls the Freemont police."

"How long would it take them to respond?" she asked.

"As long as it takes them to respond to a 911 call. The idea is for the alarm to warn you if an area of your house, namely a window or door, is breached. In the middle of the night, you could sleep through someone trying to get into your clinic. The alarm would alert you."

Ella stared at Zach for a moment and then nodded. "I see your point. The receptionist who works for me is married to an electrician. He might be able to install a system."

"The sooner the better," Zach added.

"What if the Amish decide I'm not someone they want treating their children?"

He didn't understand her logic. "Because they'll see the alarm system?"

"Yes, and because of the shots that were fired today. Am I being foolish?"

"Only if you don't think of your own safety. The Amish may not even hear about the break-in at your clinic or the shooter in the woods."

She sighed as she picked up a pile of files and returned them to the cabinet. "Obviously you haven't been around the Amish. Even without modern conveniences like telephones and social media, news travels."

A key turned in the door, surprising both of them. Zach stepped protectively in front of Ella.

The woman who pushed her way inside was dressed in light blue scrubs that covered her full figure. The embroidered emblem on her uniform read Children's Care

Clinic. Evidently the newcomer—in her midforties, with rosy cheeks and pink lipstick—worked for the doc.

The nurse opened her arms and headed straight for Ella. Zach had to step aside to keep from being run over.

"I've been so worried," the woman gushed. "The police stopped at my house. They took my fingerprints and wanted to make sure I hadn't given the clinic key to anyone. Why didn't you call me?"

She wrapped Ella in a warm embrace.

"I'm fine, Wendy. You shouldn't have worried. I planned to call you, but somehow time got away from me."

"You were hurt and fought for your life? That's the story I heard."

"I wasn't injured, but Mary Kate Powers is in the hospital at Fort Rickman with a gunshot wound."

The woman pulled back, her eyes wide. "I had no idea. Tell me the twins weren't hurt."

"They're fine and staying with their grandparents."

Seemingly, the newcomer posed no threat. Zach stepped closer, and Ella introduced him to Nurse Wendy Kelsey.

"You're from post?" she asked, after hearing "CID" in the introduction.

"That's right." Zach nodded. "I'm working with the Freemont police. How did you learn about the attack?"

"The cop who took my prints said someone broke in and attacked Ella." Wendy patted her chest as she glanced at her employer. "I called your cell but couldn't get an answer. I decided to drive here and see if I could find out what happened."

"Someone ransacked the clinic this morning. Special Agent Swain is helping me tidy the clutter."

Wendy stuck her purse in one of the cabinets and hung up the sweater she was wearing. "Why don't you fix yourself a cup of tea and let me get to work."

Ella visibly relaxed. "That sounds perfect. Thank you, but I'll brew some coffee and be back with cups for everyone." She turned to Zach. "You take yours black?"

"Black and strong."

Ella headed to the hallway that led to her residence and returned ten minutes later with three steaming cups. The hot brew was exactly what Zach needed.

He and Wendy quickly cleaned up the remaining items, and the nurse had the place looking even better by the time he had finished his coffee.

"I'll call the patients who have appointments and see if they can come another day," she said. "In fact, I suggest the clinic remain closed through the weekend and open again on Monday."

"Our Amish patients don't have phones, Wendy. How can you contact them?" Ella asked.

"The twins were the only children scheduled for today. I'll call their grandmother and cancel their visit and reschedule the other non-Amish patients. Thankfully, you don't have any appointments with Amish patients for the rest of the week."

"That's a good idea." Zach glanced at Ella. "The case may be solved by Monday. Plus it gives you more time to heal and gain your strength."

"You might be right." She stepped closer to the nurse. "I stopped by the Landerses' house this morning and checked on the twins. They're both doing well."

"You've made a difference in those girls' lives." Wendy turned to Zach. "If Ella hadn't diagnosed their condition, they wouldn't have survived. That assured many of the local folks, when they saw the twins improve."

The nurse continued to share stories about the positive impact Ella had made on the community until the doc waved off her praise. "I did what any physician would do.

Fortunately, my husband's work provided the answers. Otherwise everything could have been very different."

She went to the window and pulled back the curtains. "The sun is shining. I want a little of that to brighten the clinic. You've both done so much to make it better. Thank you, Wendy."

Turning to Zach, Ella said, "I didn't expect a special agent in law enforcement to be so handy. The dead bolts will keep me secure and give me peace of mind."

Looking at her nurse, she asked, "Would you call Beth and inquire if her husband can install a security alarm for me?"

Wendy nodded. "Good idea. I'm on it."

Glancing out the window, Zach noticed a red pickup racing along the road past the clinic. The tires squealed as it turned into the farm next door.

"Looks like Levi Miller has company," he said, heading for the door.

Ella peered out the window. "It's Mary Kate's husband. What's he up to?"

"I'll check it out."

"I'll go with you," Ella stated. "I want to find out about Mary Kate's condition."

"You should stay here," Zach insisted.

"Nonsense." She opened a cabinet and pulled out a black medical bag. "I need to check on Levi's wife, as well."

He glanced at the bag. "Doctors still make house calls?"

She nodded. "They do in rural Georgia."

"We'll take my car."

Ella was puzzled. "But the Millers live next door."

"And someone tried to shoot you in your backyard."

She nodded, realizing he was right. Her eyes fell on the weapon he carried under his jacket. She couldn't deny the sense of security that knowing Zach was armed gave her.

"You'll protect me." She said it as a statement.

"Of course I will."

The confidence and assurance of his answer warmed her heart. She'd be safe with the special agent. At least, that was her hope.

SIX

Some folks might call the doc headstrong. Zach thought independent was more apropos. Had her need to prove herself gotten her in trouble? Or had the attack at the clinic been a result of a strong-willed doctor trying to push her way into someplace she wasn't wanted?

Last night, she'd been scared and needing reassurance when she'd stepped into his arms, after remembering the gun the attacker had brandished.

What had made Zach pull her into his embrace? He wasn't one to be swayed by a pretty face or silky hair and big eyes, yet he'd reacted without thinking.

Everything within him had wanted to comfort Ella and protect her. Not because she was a doctor. He didn't have much use for physicians, especially country docs, like the one who had made a tragic error that had led to his mother's death.

No, the woman he'd seen last night had been Ella Jacobsen, without the physician facade. Perhaps she hadn't realized the vulnerability she'd revealed to him at that moment. Something that was at the heart of who she was when she didn't try to be in charge.

Ella paused momentarily by the door to glance at her reflection in a wall mirror. Gingerly, she touched the puffy bruise on her cheek and frowned.

A number of bruises were all too evident in the sunlight steaming through the window. The sight of her injuries made Zach's gut tighten. No one should ever hurt a woman. Seeing the marks on her face and another bruise on her arm enhanced his desire to find the heinous individual who had caused Ella so much pain. Unless the attacker was found and apprehended, he'd be back again.

"I'm ready," she said. "Let's pay the Millers a visit."

"You haven't slept, Doc. Sure you wouldn't rather stay here?"

She straightened her shoulders. "You haven't slept, either, Special Agent Swain."

"Zach, remember?"

Some of her bravado faltered, and she smiled, causing a jolt of energy to take him by surprise. He'd thought Ella Jacobsen was pretty last night, but in the light of day, he realized how wrong he'd been. She was beautiful.

"We'll go together," Zach said. "But do me a favor and follow my lead."

"Of course."

Was she being sincere or condescending?

Clutching her doctor's bag, she opened the front door and stepped outside. Hurriedly, she descended the stairs and walked with determined steps to his vehicle. As much as it seemed like a waste of fuel to drive such a short distance, Zach needed to keep Ella safe.

After parking in the Millers' driveway, he stepped from the car and flicked his gaze to the wooded area behind the house and the pasture in the distance, looking for anything that might spell danger.

Before he could round the hood to open the passenger door, Ella had stepped out and, bag in hand, was racing toward the house.

The woman had stamina, Zach would give her that.

"Are you in a hurry?" he asked, falling into step beside her.

"Just focused on seeing if Sarah is okay. I've got a strange feeling that all of this hubbub has taken its toll on her. She's in her early twenties and has been racked with morning sickness for the last six months."

"I thought it eased up after the first three."

"That's usually the case, but some women continue to have problems into the second and even third trimester. Sarah has lost weight instead of gaining, and she's anxious about the health of her child. She and Levi lost a baby at seven months. That was before I arrived in the area. As you can imagine, she's worried this baby might have problems."

"I'm sure having a doctor next door has eased her worry."

"I wish that was the case. Instead, I've opened up other concerns."

"You mean the incidents of genetically acquired diseases that the Amish carry?"

"That's it exactly. Some of them would rather not know about the complications."

"Are any upset enough to break into your clinic?"

Ella turned to stare at him quizzically. "You must not understand the Amish or you wouldn't suspect them."

"I understand human nature and the fact that bad people can be found in any population. Even the Amish."

"They're a peaceful people who put their faith in God."

"Perhaps that's their mistake."

She narrowed her gaze. "You don't believe in God?"

"I believe there is a God, but I believe man is responsible for his own actions. I also know that some men and women live by another rule, other than the golden rule. Evil exists. I'm sure it exists even in the Amish community."

Nearing the house, Zach turned his focus to sounds that were floating from the side of the property. Sounds of an argument.

"Stay here, Doc."

He hurried ahead and made a wide arc around the house to better see the source of the raised voices. Hugh Powers and Levi Miller came into view. The corporal was waving his hands in the air, visibly upset. Levi kept his at his sides and was responding to Hugh in what sounded like a calm and steady voice. Zach moved closer to hear more of their conversation.

"Do you understand what I'm saying?" The muscular military guy jabbed his finger against Levi's chest. "You have no business hanging around Mary Kate."

"I would not hurt your wife," Levi replied, his voice even and his body relaxed.

Zach admired the young lad for keeping his cool.

Hugh raised a fist. "You know what happens to people who harm anyone I love?"

"Corporal Powers," Zach called, stepping closer.

Hugh's brow furrowed. "What are you doing here?"

"That's the question I wanted to ask you. This is Levi Miller's property. Did he invite you onto his land?"

"He invited my wife." Hugh's voice was laced with anger. He steeled his jaw, turned his gaze back to the Amish man and pointed a finger at Levi's suspenders. "You may look peaceful with the funny clothes you and your friends wear, but you're hiding your true nature."

"I have nothing to hide."

"You need to pay for your transgressions." The soldier's eyes narrowed. "For your sins, Mr. Miller. My father-in-law told me what you did to my wife. Then you disappeared, hiding out in your closed community that claims to be holier than thou. But in reality you're a pervert who preys on an unsuspecting woman."

Zach moved closer. "We can discuss your suspicions, Corporal Powers, but in a less heated manner. Take a step back, and give Mr. Miller some space."

"He doesn't deserve space."

"Do you need to go to CID headquarters, where we can discuss this at length? That's not going to help Shelly or Stacey. Or your wife."

At the mention of his wife, the soldier's head drooped. He turned and walked away from both of them, his shoulders shaking.

Levi glanced at Zach but said nothing.

Zach gave the soldier a minute to pull himself together, then stepped to the man's side and touched his back. "You're upset, Hugh. I understand that you want to find the person who hurt your wife, but you need to work with law enforcement and not take things into your own hands. If you harm or even antagonize Mr. Miller, I'll be forced to haul you in. That's not what you want."

The big guy pursed his lips and then blew out a breath. "I can't stand seeing Mary Kate hurt like that. She's hooked up to tubes and looks like she's going to die." He stared at Zach. "I saw enough death when I was deployed. I didn't expect to come home to see my wife bloody and beaten. Do you understand why I want to fix her pain and make everything right?"

"Of course I understand, but you've got to let law enforcement handle the investigation." Zach passed his business card to the soldier. "I gave you my card last night, but here's another one. Keep this in your barracks or your truck, and call me whenever you think of anything that might have bearing on the investigation. Or call if you want to check on what we've uncovered. I won't hold back the truth from you, but you have to be forthright with me, as well."

The soldier nodded. "I told you everything I knew last night."

"Then why did you come here? What were you hoping to accomplish?"

"I...I wanted to warn Miller to stay away from my wife."

Zach glanced at Levi and then turned back to Corporal Powers. "What makes you think Levi was interested in Mary Kate?"

"My father-in-law saw them together more than once."

"Before you redeployed home?"

"That's right. He was worried about Mary Kate. Worried about her safety."

From what Zach knew about Mary Kate's father, the old man was prone to jumping to the wrong conclusion, yet there had to be some semblance of truth in what he'd told his son-in-law.

"Is everything okay?"

Ella's voice.

Zach turned to see her standing at the side of the house. She walked toward Levi. "How's Sarah?"

"She's sick again, and it troubles her. Her father says it's *Gott's* will, but she worries that it means something's wrong with the baby."

"I told you the nausea had nothing to do with the baby's condition. It's caused by the hormones Sarah's body is producing because she is pregnant."

"Her mother had no sickness, and she delivered healthy children."

"But Sarah is her own person. Every pregnancy is different."

Levi's gaze darkened. "Yet Sarah was sick the first time."

"Again, Levi, that's her body's response to the pregnancy and doesn't have anything to do with the well-being of this baby."

"I want to believe you, Dr. Jacobsen, but I still worry."

"I understand." Ella patted his arm. "You love your wife, but you can believe me, Levi."

"I believe in *Gott's* will. He may take this child like he took the first. Perhaps because of my mistake years ago."

Ella glanced at Zach and then back at Levi. "Your mistake?"

"I was young and headstrong. My father said a man needs to keep his eyes to himself. He told me *Gott* would find a righteous woman. Instead I looked elsewhere."

Hugh turned, his face flushed with anger, and pointed to Levi. "Are you blaming Mary Kate for what happened? It was your fault, Miller. You're a hypocrite. You told her you loved her, that you'd never leave her and that you could have a life together, but those were all lies."

Sadness washed over Levi's face. "I did not lie."

"You didn't do anything to help her. You lousy—"

Zach grabbed the soldier's arm. "Let's all take a deep breath."

Hugh stopped and shook his head. "I'm not going to hurt him. I don't touch men who don't fight back and who don't protect the woman they say they love."

He glared at Levi. "You lied to Mary Kate. You told her you loved her and that you wanted to marry her. She was young, and she trusted you, Miller. That was her mistake. Your mistake was to get her pregnant."

Hugh jerked his arm from Zach's hold. "I'm going home to be with my daughters. The precious children you abandoned, Miller. I adopted them. They bear my name and they're my children. So stay away from them, and stay away from my wife."

The soldier walked purposefully back across the yard. Zach let him go. As the red pickup pulled out of the driveway, Zach phoned Sergeant Abrams and passed on what Hugh had just revealed.

"Might be a good idea to head to the grandparents' home and question both Mr. Landers and Hugh," he added. "Find out if either of them own a rifle. I'll stay here and talk to Levi Miller. Did you learn anything from him earlier?"

"He seems to be on the up-and-up."

"That's what I wanted to hear."

"I've got a patrol car in the vicinity of the grandparents' house. My guys will make sure Corporal Powers stays put until I have a chance to question him."

Relieved that the Freemont police would check on the Landers family, Zach disconnected and glanced over his shoulder at Ella, who stood next to Levi.

"I didn't hurt her," the Amish man insisted, as Zach moved back to them. "I would never hurt Mary Kate." Levi's voice was tight with emotion. "I loved her. It wasn't as her husband said."

"What about now, Mr. Miller?" Zach asked. "Do you still have feelings for Mary Kate?"

"Levi?" A frail voice sounded from the small, wood-frame house.

Zach glanced at the door, where a young woman— a very pregnant woman—stood staring at her husband.

"Are you all right, Levi?" she asked.

"*Yah*, Sarah. I am fine. Do not worry."

Her hands rubbed her belly, and her eyes filled with sadness as if she'd heard everything that had transpired.

The strain visible on Ella's face revealed that she, too, understood the gravity of the situation. Had she known all along that Levi was the girls' biological father?

The disease Ella had diagnosed was found most often among the Amish. Zach should have put two and two together last night, but he'd been so focused on the doctor that he'd failed to realize what seemed so obvious today.

Had Levi attacked Mary Kate out of anger because she'd come back to Freemont and disrupted his life, perhaps causing his wife untold anxiety? Or was he after the medical records that revealed the disease the twins had inherited? Information in their file could point to their Amish background and could even mention their biological father. If that were the case, then Ella had kept that information from Zach, as well.

He flicked his gaze to her, berating himself for being so easily swayed. He didn't trust doctors, not even pretty ones with bruised cheeks and big eyes—eyes that stared at him now as if he was the one who had brought pain to this small Amish community.

Do no harm. Ella tried to practice medicine according to the Hippocratic Oath, but she had caused pain and suffering. Had coming to Georgia been a mistake?

She read distrust and questions in the special agent's eyes as he continued to stare at her. Did he blame her, even as she was blaming herself?

"Levi?" Once again, Sarah called to her husband.

"Everything is all right," he said, as if hoping to reassure her. One look at Sarah's face and it was evident his words had no effect on calming her unease.

The *clip-clop* of horse hooves caused them all to look toward the road. A bearded man sat holding the reins as an Amish buggy passed. He nodded to Levi.

Zach watched as the buggy continued on. Then, turning, he studied the wooded area behind the house and the pastures to one side. His expression of concern made Ella realize that standing outside in the open exposed all of them.

"We need to finish this discussion inside," Levi said,

no doubt picking up on the special agent's worry. "Please, come into my house." He motioned them toward the door.

"Sarah can come to the clinic with me," Ella suggested. "If you men want to talk in private."

"No." Levi shook his head. "Sarah needs to hear what I will say." Again, he pointed to the door. "Please."

Ella hurried up the steps to where Sarah stood. "You're not feeling well today?" She took the Amish woman's hand.

"Levi says I must place my trust in *Gott*, and I do, but I still worry about our baby."

"I brought my medical bag. Let's go to your bedroom. I'll check the baby's heartbeat."

"That will bring me comfort."

Seeing the worry in Sarah's drawn face, Ella rubbed the younger woman's shoulder, hoping to offer reassurance. "I told you everything looks good."

"I believe what you said with my head, but not with my heart. Do you understand?"

"I understand your desire for a child. What happened with your first pregnancy does not mean that it will happen again. This second child is gaining weight and growing. She or he will be healthy and will bring you and Levi joy for the rest of your lives."

"You bring me hope." A weak smile formed on Sarah's thin lips. "May I offer you a slice of apple pie?"

"That sounds wonderful." Ella glanced at Zach. "I'm sure the special agent would like some, as well. Let the men talk while I check the baby. Then we can enjoy your pie."

Entering the bedroom, Ella found her gaze drawn to the beautiful quilt that covered the bed. The workmanship was so detailed. The colors were muted, as was the Amish way, but the intricate pattern was like a work of art.

"Did you create this quilt?" Ella asked.

"Before Levi and I married. I did it as an act of love."

"You're an artist, Sarah."

"My sister taught me to stitch. She is a good teacher, but the praise goes to *Gott*. He creates the beauty in my mind before I sew the pieces together."

"You're much too humble," Ella said, as she helped her stretch out on the bed. Sarah's hands clenched as Ella listened to the baby's heartbeat.

Once satisfied, she helped the pregnant woman to a sitting position and assured her that the beat was strong. Relief spread over Sarah's sweet face and a twinkle returned to her eyes. Together the two of them hurried back to the kitchen, where the men sat at the handcrafted table.

Zach was bent over a notebook, scribbling something onto a page. "When did you first meet Hugh Powers?" he asked, then looked up, distracted, as the women entered the room.

Levi stared at Sarah as she passed the table and hurried to where the pie sat on the counter. Ella stood close by, ready to help serve.

"He's only recently come back from the Middle East," Levi said. "I never met him, but I was riding in my buggy near their house not long ago and saw him get out of his truck."

"Did he see you?"

"He glanced my way. Mary Kate was with him, but I did not see the girls."

"Have you had any connection with the twins?"

Levi shook his head. "Their mother asked that I stay out of their lives. She does not want to confuse them with two fathers."

Zach started to respond and then glanced at Sarah, who was pulling plates from the cabinet.

Levi must have read his thoughts. "It is all right that you continue to ask your questions, Special Agent Swain.

I told you, Sarah and I do not have secrets. I have confessed my sin. The bishop says *Gott* has forgiven my transgressions."

"Is there anyone who might be holding a grudge? Perhaps a family member of yours?" Again, Zach glanced at Sarah. "Or someone in your wife's family?"

"Her brother, Daniel, was not happy when we married. He did not think I would be a faithful husband."

"Is he still antagonistic?" Zach asked.

"He moved to Alabama, so I cannot speak for him," Levi said. "But the Amish do not hold grudges."

Sarah turned from cutting the pie. "Daniel was protective of me when we were children. It is hard for him to let go of that responsibility."

"Protective of you in what way, if you don't mind me asking?" Zach said.

"In the Amish home, the father is the disciplinarian, and he has total authority. That is usually not a problem when a man has love in his heart."

"You're saying that your father was a stern authoritarian?"

"My mother died three months after their last child was born. My father could never get over her loss."

"Where are you in the birthing order?"

Sarah's eyes turned serious. "I am the youngest."

"Your father took his grief and frustration out on you?" Zach voice was laced with understanding.

"He said I was a difficult child."

"Where does your father live now?"

"On a small farm not far from here."

Zach looked at Levi. "Would your father-in-law become violent and do Mary Kate harm?"

The Amish man pursed his lips. Finally, he said, "I cannot see anyone harming a woman."

"Do I detect a bit of hesitation on your part, Levi, in answering my question?"

"I do not want to falsely represent Sarah's father. He is a proud man, and he forbade her to marry me."

Ella's heart went out to the fragile woman with the soft voice who stood with her back to the counter.

"Sarah, you married Levi against your father's will?" Zach asked.

She stepped to the table and placed her hand on Levi's shoulder. "I love my husband. He is a *gut* man. In youth, we often make mistakes. Levi had not yet been baptized. He was on his *rumspringa*. It is a time for the youth to explore other ways. He returned to the Amish community and was baptized. *Gott* accepted him. So did I."

Sarah glanced at Ella as if to gain support. "Although a daughter is to obey her father, my *datt* was making bad decisions for my future," the Amish wife continued. "I went to the bishop. Thankfully, he listened. Levi told him of his love for me, and the bishop gave us his blessing. This is something I have never regretted."

"I know this is a difficult question, Sarah." Zach hesitated, as if to let the seriousness of what he was about to say settle in. "Do you think your father is capable of harming Mary Kate?"

The young woman gripped her husband's shoulder. Levi raised his hand and touched her fingers, offering encouragement.

"I do not doubt that my father could and would do physical harm to Mary Kate. As he ages, his mind becomes more twisted. He could think that getting rid of her would erase everything that happened, including having a daughter who disrespects his authority."

"Is that what he's said?" Zach asked.

"He has said this, yes." She wiped her hands on her apron, then stepped back to the counter and lifted a knife to cut the pie. "Perhaps you are hungry and would like something to eat?"

Ella looked at Zach and nodded almost imperceptibly. Thankfully, he picked up on her subtle cue.

"Thank you, Sarah. I would enjoy a piece of pie."

"*Gut.*" The young woman's face broke into a strained smile. "We will eat."

"Could you give me directions to find Sarah's father?" Zach asked Levi as Sarah cut the pie.

He drew a map on Zach's tablet. "My father-in-law's farm is off Amish Road. The turn is hard to see when the leaves are on the trees. He likes to remain secluded. Be careful. He has a shotgun and will use it."

"I thought the Amish were pacifists," Zach stated.

"That does not stop my father-in-law from brandishing his hunting rifle."

A chill wrapped around Ella's heart as she saw the concern on Zach's face.

"Do you have a rifle?" he asked Levi.

"I do, but I only use it for hunting."

"Could you get it for me?"

Sarah turned abruptly to stare at her husband. Fear flashed in her eyes.

"Is something wrong?" Zach asked.

She shook her head. "Everything is fine."

Levi slowly rose from the table and went to the back of the house. He returned with the rifle and passed it to Zach, who looked through the barrel. "When was the last time you cleaned your rifle?"

"After I went hunting," Levi said. "Probably two weeks ago."

"You haven't used it since then?"

"That is right. I have not used it since."

"Then there's a problem." Zach touched the chamber. A black, powdery smudge dirtied his finger. "This doesn't look like cleaning oil to me. It looks more like gunpowder residue."

He stared at the younger man. "The gun's been fired since you cleaned it, Levi. Either you're mistaken about your cleaning routine or you've fired the rifle in the last two weeks."

Levi stared back at him but didn't respond.

Sarah gripped the counter as if to regain her balance, then covered her mouth with her hand and ran from the room.

Ella glared at Zach for half a second, uncertain what had just happened. Surely he didn't believe that Levi had viciously attacked her or Mary Kate. Nor had Levi fired on Ella today. Then she remembered what Zach had told her earlier.

Evil could be found anywhere, even in the Amish community.

SEVEN

Ella followed Sarah into her room and found the young woman sitting on the bed, head in her hands. As she stepped closer, she heard the deep intake of air and then faint sobs as Sarah began to cry. Ella sat next to her on the thick quilt.

"Sarah…" She kept her voice low. "Nothing is worth your tears. Tell me what's wrong."

The young mother-to-be shook her head.

Ella hesitated a moment, giving her time to work through the swell of emotions that had obviously over-powered her.

"I'm your doctor, Sarah, but I'm also a neighbor and a friend. I won't share the information unless you give me permission. You can trust me."

"I…I know." Her voice was weak and fraught with feeling.

"Is this about Levi and the gun?"

She shook her head again. "Not Levi."

"But it concerns the rifle?"

Sarah nodded. She dug for the handkerchief tucked in her sleeve and wiped her cheeks. "Levi worries about me when I am alone. He has always been protective of me, but even more so now because of the baby. Sometimes I think he worries that someone will do me harm."

"He wants to keep you safe because he loves you," Ella said encouragingly. "That's not a bad thing."

"I know that is true, and I love him and always want to do what he asks of me."

"I'm sure you're a wonderful wife. Levi is blessed to have you."

Sarah continued to hang her head, as if ashamed of what she was about to reveal. "My father said I was a fool to marry a man who loved another."

Ella rubbed her hand over the woman's slender shoulders. "But you said that your father does not have a loving heart. He might not have approved of any man you chose to marry."

Sarah's brow furrowed for a moment and then she nodded. "Perhaps you are right. Although a child is to obey her parents, especially her father. I tried to be a dutiful daughter."

"You shouldn't worry about your father."

"He frightens me at times. Especially since his mind is failing him. His anger has increased."

Ella glanced down at the intricately pieced quilt and wished the pieces of information Sarah had provided would fit together half as well. "Did your father have something to do with Levi's gun?" she asked.

"No, but there was a man…"

The new detail made Ella's heart lurch with concern. Again, she patted the young woman's shoulders. "Tell me what happened, Sarah."

"Two days ago, Levi went to town. He wanted to find some work to do for extra money so we could better prepare for the baby. He worries that there might be a problem and the baby may need special help at the hospital."

"I told you that I'd deliver the baby and wouldn't charge you."

"That is right, and we are so grateful. But you also

mentioned that the baby could need special care, if..." She dropped her head into her hands and started crying again.

"Sarah, you need to be strong. I told you the pregnancy is going well. The baby is growing and gaining weight. The heartbeat is good."

With a decided sniff, Sarah wiped her eyes and raised her head. "Levi says that I fret too much, but I know he worries, too. He is worried about how to provide for another mouth to feed." She looked around. "Our house is small."

"Your Amish neighbors will help."

"Some will. Others, like my brother and father, will not help. They cannot accept Levi."

"But your faith tells them to forgive."

"Some precepts are harder to accept, and some people think they are above the teachings and the truth that we hold so dear."

"It's the same in all cultures, I'm afraid," Ella answered, thinking of the people in Carlisle who had become aloof after Quin died. Perhaps because he had taken his own life; perhaps because they didn't understand his work, or the way he had grown more and more distant.

"That is why I didn't tell Levi." Sarah spoke slowly, her voice little more than a whisper.

Leaning closer, Ella asked, "Tell Levi what?"

"About the man I saw. Two days ago. The sun was setting, and darkness was settling over the land. I looked out the window and saw a man walking from the stand of trees."

"The trees behind our houses?" The same area that the shots had come from today.

"That is right. A dirt road runs along the property line. I thought he must have come from that road."

"Who was it?"

"His dress was *fancy*. He wore denim pants and a

hooded fleece shirt. The hood covered his hair, but he also wore a hat with a wide bill—" She raised her hand to indicate how it would fit.

"A baseball cap," Ella suggested.

"Yes. It was low on his brow so I could not see his face. He hurried toward our house."

Ella tried to think where she had been at that time of day. "Was I at home?"

"I heard you leave earlier. Maybe you were in town?"

She nodded, remembering her schedule. "I didn't have patients and went to the grocery store in Freemont. I got home after dark, but I didn't see anyone hanging around."

"He was gone by then. I watched him walk around my property. He peered in one of the windows as if he wanted to see if anyone lived here."

"I'm sure you were frightened." Without a phone, Sarah couldn't call for help.

"Levi told me never to touch his gun. He worried I could hurt myself."

"But you were afraid," Ella volunteered.

"I was. The man tried the front door. I feared he would go to the back door and try to get inside. When he came around the house, I opened the door a bit and yelled at him to leave."

Ella was surprised the young woman had had the courage to do so.

"He took a step closer. I did not think he would go away, so I fired Levi's rifle." She looked at Ella. "Not at him, but at the ground. He ran to the woods. I watched for him to return, but he never did."

"You didn't tell Levi?"

"I planned to, but Levi was discouraged when he got home. He had found no jobs, and I could see the worry in his eyes. He said he'd had a strange feeling that something was wrong at home. He'd hurried back and wanted to arrive before dark, but a wheel on the buggy had a problem, and he had to fix it along the way."

The woman searched Ella's gaze as if for acceptance. "I could not tell him about the man or that I had used his rifle. I did not think he would find out. I thought the next time he went hunting he would not check his gun first, but I was wrong. Now I fear the special agent from Fort Rickman thinks Levi is the person who shot at you today."

"You need to tell both men what happened."

Sarah nodded. "I should not have kept the truth from my husband."

"Can you describe the man?"

"Only what he was wearing, as I told you."

"Was there anything about his face?"

Sarah shook her head. "His hat was so low that I could not see much. Plus I was frightened and shaking. When I think back, everything is blurred."

"Which is how I feel about last night. I can't recall what the attacker looked like. He had a flashlight that nearly blinded me with its brightness, but I should be able to remember more."

"We have both tried to block out evil that has tried to touch our lives." Sarah rubbed her hands over her arms as if she was cold. "I must tell Levi and Special Agent Swain."

"You don't have to worry about Zach. He's a good man, just like Levi."

"I can see it in his eyes. You have been friends for a long time?"

Ella was surprised by the question. "No, we just met last night. Why do you ask?"

"The way he looks at you. His gaze carries more with it, as if you share a special bond."

Ella stared at Sarah for a long moment and then stood, unable to make sense of the tangle of emotions tugging at her heart. "You probably noticed his inquisitive nature. He investigates crime and wants to get to the bottom of every situation. That's what you see in his gaze."

The girl shook her head. "No, there is more. But now I must tell my husband what I have kept from him and ask his forgiveness."

Ella opened the bedroom door and was the first to step into the kitchen. Zach raised his gaze and stared at her. A feeling stirred deep within her that made her breath catch in her throat.

She pulled her eyes away and turned as Sarah walked toward her husband.

"Levi, I must tell you something that I have kept from you."

His face was creased with concern. "Is it the baby?" He rose and went to her.

"The baby is fine." She glanced at Ella. "At least, that is what our nice neighbor keeps telling me. But there is something else. We will sit and have pie, and I will explain what happened."

"Why don't you begin," Ella suggested. "I'll serve the pie." As she cut slices, she watched Levi's face, which was so filled with love for his wife. He was concerned about her health, and hearing about the stranger who had tried their front door made him turn pale with fear for her safety.

Zach leaned across the table, taking in everything the young woman shared. Just as Ella had mentioned in the bedroom, he wanted a full description of the stranger and any other details Sarah could remember.

Levi was too distraught to eat and kept holding his wife's hand and apologizing for returning home late that night.

Zach asked a number of questions, obviously hoping

to unlock Sarah's memory, but she could think of nothing more than what she had told Ella.

Ella picked at the pie. The apples were green, but Sarah had sweetened them with just the right amount of sugar. Still, Ella's stomach tightened, and she had no appetite. The few bites she ate were to comfort the young wife who wanted to please everyone.

Zach turned again to stare at Ella. As if reading his thoughts, she realized the stranger had been canvassing the area before he stopped by her clinic.

Was his visit in any way involved with Levi and Sarah? Or was it about Ella, the patient records she kept on hand or the treatment she provided to the local Amish community?

What was going on in this once-idyllic part of Georgia? Ella tried to read Zach's gaze, but all she saw were questions about who she was and what had happened to her peaceful life.

"You're quiet," Zach said from the driver's seat as they left the Millers' property. The map Levi had drawn to his father-in-law's farm lay between them.

"Just thinking back to everything that's happened," Ella said. "If I hadn't come to Freemont, Levi and Sarah wouldn't be in the middle of an investigation."

"It isn't your fault. Besides, Levi is merely a person of interest. So is Mary Kate's husband. After Abrams talks to her father, Mr. Landers might be, as well. Any investigation has a number of folks who need to be questioned. That doesn't mean they're guilty or involved in the crime."

"Then you don't suspect Levi?"

"I don't know what to think. He and his wife seem to have a loving marriage in spite of his earlier relationship with Mary Kate. She's moved on, as well."

"Was she the reason for the clinic break-in? Did the assailant want to do her harm?"

"Perhaps. Still, every angle needs to be followed. What's in the twins' medical record that might cause someone to want those files?"

"You know that's not something I can share. I'm sure you're well aware of the Privacy of Information Act. Information between a physician and her patients is privileged."

"I'm not asking about any psychological evaluations, Doc. I just need to know some general facts. I'm sure the file mentions the genetic condition you uncovered."

Ella refused to comment.

"What about the biological father? Was Levi's name in the files?"

She sighed but failed to respond.

"Ella, I'm not interested in their medical information, per se. I need to know if the father's name was listed." Zach stared at her, feeling mildly frustrated. "I can get a court order, if you won't help me out, but I don't think what I'm asking is anything we haven't discussed with both the adoptive and biological fathers."

"You're right. Both men have been open about their role in the children's lives." She rubbed her hands together and then sighed. "Corporal Hugh Powers is listed as the adoptive father."

"So you didn't include Levi's name in the records?"

"It wasn't necessary to include anything about him. Plus, I didn't know who the birth father was, nor did I ask Mary Kate."

"Yet the disease you diagnosed has been specifically associated with Amish children."

"Perhaps I should have pressed Mary Kate to reveal the biological father, but I was more concerned about restoring the girls to health. Now that they've improved, that detail may be something that would have bearing on future children, should Mary Kate get pregnant again. You're correct in saying that the disease occurs more frequently with Amish, but it could also appear randomly in nature."

"So it isn't just an Amish disease?"

"That's right, although the incidence is much higher in the Amish community due to the limited founding families."

Zach held up his hand. "Can you backtrack a bit?"

"A certain number of Amish fled to America because of religious persecution. Those families remained close-knit and intermarried. Recessive genes that would dissipate in a larger population were enhanced within the small founding pool. My husband studied those families and the diseases they develop because of their intermarriages. If Quin were still alive, he would have traced the girls' lineage. That was his interest, but not mine."

"Still, it seems you would have wondered about the father."

"I knew Corporal Powers had adopted the girls. Mary Kate left the area before the twins were born and moved south of Savannah. She has an aunt who lives there. I'm sure the aunt provided lodging while she was pregnant. Some people think nothing of out-of-wedlock pregnancies. Other folks still don't want the information to be made public. I have a feeling Mary Kate's father was the latter."

"Has he ever mentioned knowing who the biological father was?"

"I haven't heard him talk about Levi, except what he said today. I'm sure he knew. That's probably why he is so antagonistic toward Levi."

"Mr. Landers insinuated that Mary Kate and Levi had met recently."

"I'm sure Levi wanted to find out information about his daughters. Plus he wanted to know how the condition affected the girls."

"Did he ask you about the disease?" Zach inquired.

"Only in general terms. I've drawn blood samples on both Levi and Sarah and am awaiting the test results, as I told you. With CED, both parents have to carry the gene in order for their offspring to be susceptible."

"Both parents provide a gene?" Zach pressed. "Does that mean it's recessive?"

Ella nodded. "That's right."

"So Mary Kate comes from Amish lineage?"

"I...I don't know. As I mentioned, the disease can appear in the general population, yet it's much more prevalent among the Amish."

"Did you ask Mary Kate about her background?"

"No, never." Ella let out a stiff breath and shoved her hair back from her face. "I never thought about it. My husband said I didn't have a mind for research. He must have been right. I shouldn't have missed the connection."

"You're a good doctor, Ella."

She looked embarrassed and somewhat surprised by his comment. "I appreciate the compliment, Zach, but I have a feeling you just want to lift my spirits. Besides, I don't seem to be tracking down all the information that should be important in a genetic study."

"Which sounds as tricky as a criminal investigation. Sometimes I'm too close," he admitted. "I need to step away for a moment to let my mind work without any hindrance."

He glanced at Ella and wondered if that was the problem with this investigation. Had he gotten too close to her and become blinded to the truth? Another thought stirred within him, even more disconcerting. Was he blinded by false testimony, an assortment of half lies or innuendos that didn't add up?

In military circles, he was considered a top-notch special agent, but this case was different. Had he changed? For the better? Or for the worse?

EIGHT

"There's the turn." Ella pointed to a narrow road almost hidden by undergrowth.

"I'm glad Levi provided directions." Zach steered his car onto the narrow lane. Deep potholes pocked the path.

"Why don't you stay in the vehicle while I meet with Mr. Fisher," Zach suggested.

"I'd feel safer with you than I would sitting alone on this desolate road."

The dirt track meandered through dense underbrush. Overhanging limbs batted at the car.

"I'd hate to travel this road in a buggy," Ella admitted.

"Perhaps there's another entrance that's less of a hazard."

"Then I suggest we take that route home."

Zach laughed. The sound filled the car and bolstered her flagging spirits. She hadn't laughed with Quin; at least, she couldn't remember laughter. Maybe in the beginning when she'd been in love with him—or in love with being in love. Had that been the reason she'd gotten married?

Zach pointed through a break in the trees. "Looks like there's some type of a structure on the ridge."

A one-story home came into view as they rounded the bend and pulled into the clearing. The house was similar to Levi and Sarah's, but the small wooden structure was anything but welcoming. The tin roof on the front porch listed as if held upright by a few rotten two-by-fours.

"If that house were in the city, it would be condemned," Ella said as she stared through the car window. "Maybe staying in the vehicle would be a safer option."

Zach pulled into the short driveway, then backed up and turned the car around so it was facing the road. "In case we need to make a fast getaway," he explained.

"Now you've got me worried."

He winked. "Law enforcement types try to be prepared for any situation, Doc."

"After all we've been through, I'd appreciate if you'd use my name instead of my title."

He pulled the keys from the ignition and turned to stare at her. "You got it, Ella. Remember to stick by me and follow my lead. We don't want to get separated, and if I say run, we run."

"Yes, sir."

He stepped from the car and studied the house, which looked more like an abandoned shack.

"See anything?" Ella asked when she joined him.

"There." Zach pointed to a dilapidated barn that listed as much as the porch. The door hung open. "I saw movement inside."

He reached under his jacket and touched the weapon he carried on his hip. "Hello," Zach called. "Mr. Fisher?"

The door of the house creaked open, and the barrel of a rifle poked through the opening. Zach flicked his gaze back and forth between the barn and the house.

"Get behind me, Ella," he said out of the side of his mouth.

She hesitated.

"Now."

Ella did as he asked, but peered around him when the

door opened a bit wider. A man stepped onto the porch. He wore typical Amish clothing and had a gray beard that added volume to his gaunt cheeks.

"He doesn't look very friendly," she said under her breath.

"Nor is he interested in providing a warm welcome." Zach squared his shoulders and stared at the old man. "I thought the Amish had big hearts and a love of God and neighbor."

Ella stepped a bit closer. "I'm guessing Sarah's father is an exception to the rule."

"Mr. Fisher?" Zach called again.

"Get off my land."

"Sir, we come as friends. I'd like to talk to you. I'm an officer of the law and work with the Criminal Investigation Division at Fort Rickman. If you step onto your porch, I can show you my identification."

"I have nothing to do with the army."

"I've brought Dr. Jacobsen." Zach pointed over his shoulder. "She has a clinic not far from here and treats Amish families. Your daughter, Sarah, is one of her patients."

"Sarah disobeyed me."

"Sir, she and Levi are expecting a child," Ella interjected. "Your grandchild."

"She lost one child, which proved *Gott* was upset with her and didn't approve of the choices she made."

"I'd like to get a family history from you, sir. That would help assure a safe delivery for your grandchild."

"Did you have anything to do with the last baby? The baby who died?"

Ella shook her head as she peered around Zach. "No, sir. I lived in Pennsylvania at the time. I'm a widow, Mr. Fisher. Sarah said you lost your wife some years ago. I know how hard that can be. My husband worked with

Amish families in Pennsylvania. You probably have kin from that state."

"*Yah*, that is right. But the English moved in and bought land, so we had no place to farm. I moved to Alabama with my wife, and to Georgia after she died. It is not good for a man to be alone."

"I'm sorry for your loss, sir, but I want to help Sarah and your grandchild. Please, put down your gun and talk to us."

The old man hesitated for a long moment.

"Mr. Fisher, I'm coming to you, sir." Zach took a step forward. "We can talk on the porch."

"Be careful," Ella whispered.

"He's thinking, and that's a good sign. I want him to know that we won't do him harm."

The old man sighed heavily, then lowered his gun and propped it against the wall. "I will talk to you, but not because of Sarah. For the baby, I will do this. The child deserves life."

"You've made a wise decision," Ella offered. She stepped around Zach and climbed the steps. The old man motioned for them to sit in the swing, while he settled into a rocker.

"Sir, you're not alone," Zach said. "Someone's in the barn. Is that a friend or family?"

"My son, Daniel. He came home to help me."

"He's been away?" Zach asked.

"*Yah*. In Alabama, where we lived when he was a baby. My daughter lives there, as well."

Ella smiled. "I'm sure your son was worried about you living alone here in the country. I know Sarah worries, too."

"Sarah should have stayed with me, then I would not be alone."

"It is right for a woman to marry, Mr. Fisher," Ella said. "I'm sure you would agree."

"To marry, *yah*. But not to marry someone her father does not approve of."

"Do you recall anyone in your family or your wife's family having children who were sickly or couldn't thrive?" Ella asked.

"You mean children who died?"

"Yes, sir, that's what I mean."

He thought for a moment. "*Mein bruder* was weak and could not eat. He became so thin and did not survive the winter."

"When was that, Mr. Fisher?"

"Years ago, when I was a boy."

"Were other family members affected?"

He shook his head. "I do not think so. What does this have to do with Sarah?"

"There are certain diseases that are seen more often among the Amish. I need to know if any of those illnesses run in your family."

"You think this baby will be born sick?"

"I hope not. But if that is the case, by knowing a family history, I can begin to treat the infant immediately."

"Another child, on my wife's side, was sickly. The child was born in the winter and did not live to spring."

"Did anyone mention the baby's cause of death?"

"The winter was cold. The father tried to cut wood to burn in the stove, but he hurt himself with his ax. He became sick, and the baby did, as well."

"I'm sorry about the loss of life."

"*Gott's* ways are not our ways."

Noticing the old man's shortness of breath, Ella glanced at Zach. He nodded, joining in her concern.

"Sir?" She patted the man's arm. "How long have you had trouble breathing?"

"I am fine." He waved her off.

Refusing to be deterred, she leaned in closer. "Your breathing is labored. As we age, our bodies sometimes need help. I'd like you to come to my clinic, Mr. Fisher. I could check your heart and your lungs."

"My heart is strong, and my breathing is fine. You can keep your medicine."

"There would be no charge. You could visit Sarah while you were there. I know she'd like to see you."

"I do not want to see my daughter or have my body examined by a woman."

"Sir," Zach interrupted. "Dr. Jacobsen is only thinking of your health."

"The Amish do not go to doctors."

"Some do," she corrected.

"Like my daughter, who does not follow the Amish ways."

"I think you'd find her very Amish, sir. She'd like to see you."

"Sir, someone broke into the doctor's clinic," Zach said. "I wondered if you'd heard of anyone who wanted to do harm to Dr. Jacobsen. Or anyone who didn't want her clinic to succeed."

"There are many who wonder why she came here."

"I came to work with the Amish, Mr. Fisher. As you may know, the nearest medical care is in Freemont. That's a long ride in a buggy."

"But we do not need doctors."

"Even the Amish get sick," she responded.

"Can you think of anyone in particular who might want to do the doctor harm?" Zach asked again.

"The Amish are peace loving people."

Who shun their family members, Ella wanted to mention. Even those who remained within the community could be excluded, such as Sarah, all because she went against her father's wishes. Mr. Fisher didn't see the hypocrisy of his statement.

Zach pointed to the rifle propped by the door. "Do you use your Winchester for hunting?"

"I do not hunt much." The old man touched his fingers to his eyes. "It is hard to see."

Ella scooted closer. "Have you had your eyes checked recently?"

"As I told you, I do not go to doctors."

"But you might need glasses," she said. "Cataracts form later in life. An eye specialist will be able to fit you for glasses. The cataracts can be removed, if your vision is compromised."

The old man ignored her and turned back to Zach. "Do you hunt?"

Evidently talk of hunting was more to his liking than any talk about his physical condition.

Zach nodded. "Although I don't have much time these days. When was the last time you shot your gun, sir? You might need to have it cleaned. I'd be happy to help you with that."

"My son helps me, as I already said. He hunts."

"Has he taken the gun recently to do some hunting?"

"*Yah*, earlier today."

Zach looked at Sarah. "Would you mind calling your son so I can talk to him?"

The old man slowly rose and walked to the edge of the porch. He put his hands up to his mouth and called, "Daniel, come."

The man Zach had noticed earlier peered from the barn.

"Come." The father motioned him forward. Turning to Zach, he added, "It is my son, Daniel."

The man walked slowly across the dirt drive and approached the house. He wore Amish trousers and a black hat pulled down on his head. He was clean shaven, which indicated he was single. But he also wore something that made Ella sit up and take note. Over his light blue shirt, he wore a navy blue hooded sweatshirt, which wasn't typical Amish clothing. Ella touched Zach's arm.

His eyes widened ever so slightly.

Ella stared at the man. Surely Sarah would recognize her brother if he had been snooping around outside her house. Had he also broken into Ella's clinic last night and then ransacked the office today and fired rounds from the woods?

She and Zach had come to the Fisher home hoping for information. But they may have found even more. They may have found the assailant.

NINE

Zach questioned Daniel while his father sat on the porch scowling. Ella had retrieved her medical bag from the car and tried to take the old man's pulse and blood pressure, but he refused to cooperate. Instead he stared at Zach and made a growling noise like an angry dog.

"Did you go near your sister's home anytime this week?" Zach asked the younger man.

"Neh."

"Did you look into Sarah's home and try the front door to see if it was locked?"

"I would not and did not."

"You went hunting today. Where were you, exactly?"

Daniel pointed to the woods. "I was in the forest. There is nothing for miles so no one stopped me, but I cannot tell you how far I went into the thicket."

"Did you shoot any game?"

"There is a bobcat. I have seen him. I fired a shot to scare him away."

"Did you wound him?"

"I did not. I shoot only that which I can eat. My father taught me well."

"Tell me about your sweatshirt," Zach said.

"I wear it when I work to keep my shirt clean."

"Is it normal for the Amish to wear fleece?"

Daniel blinked. "I am not a normal Amish man."

"Oh?" Zach hesitated before asking, "What does that mean?"

"I did not stay here, but moved back to Alabama."

"Was there a reason you left the area?"

"I needed space. Land is cheaper there."

"But you came back," Zach said.

"My father is getting older." Daniel glanced at the house. "As you can see with your own eyes, this place needs work. I came home to help him."

An altruistic cause, although Zach wondered if Daniel was telling the truth. "You are not married?"

He shook his head. "I am not."

"Isn't that unusual?"

"Are you married?" he asked Zach.

"No, I'm not."

"Do you think that's unusual?" Daniel asked.

"I'm not Amish." Zach stated the obvious.

The son sniffed. "And I'm not convinced I should remain Amish."

"You do not believe in the Amish way of life?" Zach asked.

"Living alone is difficult. If I could find a wife, I would appreciate the plain life more."

"The Freemont police will want to talk to you, Mr. Fisher."

He frowned. "I have done nothing wrong."

"Do you carry a grudge against your brother-in-law?"

"Why would I?"

"You tell me. Were you against your sister marrying Levi Miller?"

Daniel nodded. "I did not want her to marry a man who had been with a woman and conceived children out of wedlock."

"But Levi had asked for forgiveness."

"Sometimes forgiveness is difficult to give, even if the person is sorry for their wrongdoing."

Zach narrowed his gaze. "Were you ever in love?"

"I was never in love with an English woman."

From all appearances, Daniel seemed close to Levi's age. "Did you know Mary Kate when you lived here?"

"I knew who she was."

"You and Levi were friends?"

"The community was small." Daniel nodded. "I knew the other Amish children, so yes, I knew Levi."

"Did you tell him to stay away from Mary Kate?"

Daniel shrugged. "I told him she would not be good for him."

"Were you worried about Levi or worried about yourself, Daniel? Were you interested in Mary Kate?"

The man's face tightened. Zach knew he'd touched a chord. Could it be that Daniel Fisher had feelings for Mary Kate, the same girl who had fallen in love with Levi?

Vengeance wasn't the Amish way, but Mr. Fisher and his son didn't fit the mold. Daniel had prowled around the Miller home and had run away instead of identifying himself to his sister. Perhaps he'd wanted to have words with Levi, never expecting to find Sarah there without her husband.

Stepping off the porch and away from earshot, Zach called the Freemont police and spoke with Abrams, who promised to send a patrol car to the Fisher home.

In hopes of winning Mr. Fisher over, Ella encouraged him to talk about his wife and their life together. His love for Sarah became evident when he shared some of her escapades as a small child, but his mood changed when the sound of a car engine announced he had additional visitors.

He became even more upset when two officers parked in front of his property. Daniel went willingly with them to police headquarters, claiming he had nothing to hide. With Mr. Fisher's permission, the police also took his rifle for ballistics testing.

Ella encouraged the Amish man to visit her clinic for a checkup, but he merely muttered under his breath and went back into his house.

She and Zach left the farm over a different road, equally as bumpy, that led to a wooden bridge.

"On the phone, Abrams suggested I try this way out," he told her. "It's a bit shorter, although the road looks to be as bad."

"I didn't know there was a river out here."

"It feeds into the one that runs through Freemont. The bridge was built years ago, but it's still functional."

Ella looked pensive and unsettled as they crossed the bridge. "I've been thinking about what you mentioned concerning the Powers twins," she finally said.

"You mean that a recessive gene had to come from each parent in order for both girls to have the genetic condition?"

Ella cocked her head and smiled. "For a special agent, you're pretty smart."

He laughed. "You must have a low opinion of law enforcement types."

"That's not true. It's just that I picked up on your obvious antagonism toward the medical profession."

He held up his hand. "Present company excluded."

"I'm not so sure," she teased.

"Cross my heart." He traced the sign on his chest, then glanced at her and winked. "Really. You're the exception to the rule, Doc."

She rolled her eyes. "And I thought you were so affirming."

He held back a smile, trying to be sincere in spite of the frivolity of the moment. "But I meant that as a compliment, Ella. Most doctors are self-absorbed and enthralled with their own abilities. You're humble and concerned about others."

She blushed. Her obvious embarrassment warmed his heart. "I mean it, Ella."

Just that fast, the intensity of her gaze melted a brokenness he'd carried for too long. Zach kept his emotions in check. It was the way he lived life. Ever since his mother died he'd built a wall around his heart as a protective measure, so he'd never feel that overwhelming pain of separation again. The fear of being hurt had forced him to be as reclusive as old man Fisher and had cut him off from experiencing life to the full.

His cell rang, pulling him back to the investigation. Sergeant Abrams's name appeared on the monitor.

"We just left Fisher's farm," Zach said in greeting. "Your men are hauling his son in for questioning."

"I got a call filling me in," the sergeant said. "Good work tracking down both of them. If what Sarah Miller told you about her brother is true, he could be our man."

"I'm not ready to call the case closed. Did you talk to Corporal Powers?"

"I did. He wasn't happy about being detained."

"What did you uncover?" Zach asked.

"Not much," the sergeant confessed. "He's distraught about his wife. His father-in-law mentioned Levi Miller hanging around Mary Kate. Powers suspected the worst."

"So the corporal doesn't trust his wife?"

"I didn't get that impression," Sergeant Abrams said. "But he certainly doesn't trust Levi."

"Is there anything you want the military police and CID to do?"

"No more than you already are. Corporal Powers is back at the hospital, keeping vigil over his wife. Might be good to ensure he stays on post."

"I can make that happen," Zach said. "What about Mr. Landers?"

"He's got a rifle, but it's not a 30-30 caliber. Besides, he was in the ICU with his daughter when the shots were fired today. A chaplain was visiting at the time and confirmed his alibi. Leave your cell on. I'll let you know about Daniel Fisher."

"Appreciate you keeping me in the loop."

"We're in this together," the sergeant assured him.

Ella stared at Zach when he disconnected. "Are we going to talk to Mr. and Mrs. Landers?"

"Sounds like a good idea to me, unless you're too tired."

"I'm okay, just a little surprised that you didn't tell Sergeant Abrams where we were headed."

"I was thinking of your patient privilege. I trust the sergeant, but he doesn't need to know about Mary Kate's background unless it has bearing on the case."

"Thanks."

"Just doing my job."

She smiled. "You're good at what you do."

"Now I'm the one who feels a bit embarrassed. I'm not used to getting compliments from beautiful women."

Her smile faded and a look of confusion washed over her face.

He glanced at her. "You're not blushing because you don't believe what I just said."

"No one has ever called me beautiful." Her voice was low.

"Shame on everyone else then."

"You're not only affirming," she said, "but also prone to offering compliments. That's a winning combination."

"I aim to please, ma'am."

Being with Ella lifted Zach's spirits and made him feel good about himself. She was easy to talk to and affirming in her own way. It was hard to believe that no one had ever told her she was beautiful, because she was.

For a moment, as he drove through the Amish countryside, Zach forgot about the investigation. But when he turned into the Landerses' driveway, he knew he needed to keep his mind off the doctor and focus on the job at hand.

"I'd like to talk to you about the twins," Ella said when Mrs. Landers opened the door. "Special Agent Swain is with me."

"Did something happen to Mary Kate?" The older woman motioned them inside. Just as before, she wore a solid color housedress and an apron, and her hair was neatly tucked into a bun.

"As far as we know, there's been no change," Zach said. "Is you husband at the hospital?"

"Bob's in the other room with the girls. They like Grandpa to read a story to them before they take a nap."

"I'm sure that's a special time for Shelly and Stacey." Ella took a seat on the couch Mrs. Landers indicated.

"A special time for their grandfather, too." She sat next to Ella, while Zach settled in a nearby chair.

"Would you folks like coffee?"

"No, thank you," Ella said. "We're only staying a short time. I'm sure Mary Kate told you about the genetic condition the girls have."

"Of course, but they're doing well. You identified the problem, and they've improved." Mrs. Landers's smile was sincere. "God brought you into their lives, Dr. Jacobsen. They were so sick, but you saved them. I'll always be grateful."

Ella thought of the circumstances that had brought her to the Freemont area. Had God been involved?

"The girls are back to their active selves," the woman continued. "As worried as Bob and I are about Mary

Kate, it's a relief knowing Shelly and Stacey are getting stronger."

"It brings me comfort, as well, Mrs. Landers," Ella said. "Did your daughter mention that the girls' condition is usually seen in the Amish population?"

She nodded. "Mary Kate said the twins inherited the condition from their father."

Zach leaned into the conversation. "You're talking about their biological father?"

She nodded again. "Sergeant Abrams was here earlier. He probably told you about Levi Miller. The girls inherited the condition from him."

"Actually," Ella explained, "Levi provided one of the two genes necessary for the girls to have the condition. Your daughter provided a gene, as well."

The older woman's eyes widened. "I'm not sure what you're saying."

Ella explained that two recessive genes, one from each parent, were needed in order for the condition to be transmitted. "Is anyone in your family or your husband's family Amish?" she asked in conclusion.

Mrs. Landers drew in a deep breath. "Are you sure there's no other way for the girls to get the condition?"

"The disease could manifest randomly, but that's not as likely, Mrs. Landers."

Judging from her expression, Ella was certain the grandmother had something to share. To offer reassurance, she said, "Whatever is said here would be kept private." Ella looked at Zach for confirmation.

"Yes, ma'am," he quickly agreed. "I see no reason that any medical information would need to be made public. Unless, of course, it has bearing on the current investigation."

"Do you have Amish relatives?" Ella pressed.

Mrs. Landers rubbed her hands together. "I was raised

Amish. My husband lived in the neighboring town. All the teenagers hung out at a nearby lake in the summer. That's where we met and fell in love."

"Did you leave the community to marry your husband?" Ella asked.

The woman dropped her gaze. "You might say that my daughter followed in my footsteps, although she doesn't know she was conceived before we married. My father forbade me to see Bob, so I ran away."

Ella rubbed her hand over the older woman's shoulder. "That must have been difficult for you."

Mrs. Landers nodded. "Leaving my mother was hard. When Mary Kate told us she was pregnant, I felt responsible. Bob insisted she stay with his sister, who lives in Savannah. I joined them there during Mary Kate's last trimester and for some months after the twins were born, to help care for the babies. Bob visited whenever he could get away from his company."

"Is that where your daughter met Corporal Powers?" Zach asked.

Mrs. Landers nodded. "He was stationed at Fort Stewart. They met at a fund-raiser for a wounded warrior who needed medical care. By that time, Mary Kate had a job. She had rented a house and was making it on her own, with just a little help from us. We're real proud of her."

Ella offered an encouraging smile. "You should be, Mrs. Landers."

"Mary Kate admitted that she and Levi had thought they were in love. After meeting Hugh, she knew her father's decision not to let her stay with Levi had been the right one."

"Do any of your relatives have children with similar symptoms as the twins?" Ella asked.

"I wouldn't know," Mrs. Landers admitted. "I have two sisters, but I've never gone back home. I hadn't been baptized, so I wasn't formally shunned, but my father wouldn't let anyone talk to me after I defied his authority."

Which sounded like Sarah Miller's father.

"Bob and I have a son, but he's not married. Now I'm worried about any future children Mary Kate might have," the grandmother continued.

"It's doubtful they would have the condition," Ella assured her. "Unless Corporal Powers carries the gene, and that seems highly unlikely. I could do DNA testing if they want to know for sure."

Tears welled up in Mrs. Landers's eyes. "At this point, I'm not sure Mary Kate will survive. Bob and I are praying so hard for her."

Turning at the sound of footsteps, Ella saw Mr. Landers standing in the hallway. His face was ashen.

"Did we lose Mary Kate?"

Ella shook her head and stood. "No, sir. I'm sorry if we frightened you."

Mrs. Landers hurried to her husband. "The twins got sick because of my Amish background, Bob."

"What are you saying, Lucy?"

She explained about the recessive genes. "Both Levi and Mary Kate had to give a gene in order for the girls to get sick. The condition is found in the Amish, so she inherited it from my side of the family."

"The good thing is that the girls were diagnosed early and have responded to treatment," Ella said, hoping to offer encouragement.

"I still blame Levi." Mr. Landers's voice was harsh.

"No one's to blame, Mr. Landers. I'm just glad the girls responded to the treatment."

His wife patted his hand. "We'll get through this, Bob. My father always said everything that happened was God's will, but I don't think this was His doing or what He wanted for Mary Kate. Knowing God the way I do, He's not going to let anything happen to our daughter."

"They say love conquers all," Zach said as he and Ella hurried to his car. "Mrs. Landers had to sacrifice a lot to marry her husband."

Ella nodded. "I thought about Sarah Miller, who even as a married woman is worried about her father. I doubt men realize the important role they play in their daughters' lives."

"Levi seems like a loving husband," Zach mused. "And it sounds like Corporal Powers loves the twins, although right now, he's worried about his wife and focused on her."

"I can't see Mr. Landers harming his daughter."

Zach agreed. "Some of his anger dissipated when he found out about the Amish tie-in with the girls' condition. Maybe he feels responsible, just as Mrs. Landers mentioned. If they hadn't moved to this area, their daughter never would have known Levi."

"I wish Mrs. Landers could contact her Amish relatives so they could be tested."

"Perhaps you could arrange to do that through the research center in Harrisburg," Zach suggested.

Ella nodded. "I could talk to the director. Dr. Vaughn wants me to attend the event this weekend."

"Do you think that's wise?"

"I'm not sure."

Zach didn't want Ella out of his sight. He needed to convince her to stay in the Freemont area until the investigation was over, although he knew the medical symposium was important because of her husband's role in the Amish Project.

His fear was that after seeing the people with whom her husband had worked, she might not want to return to her clinic and the simple life in the Amish community.

What was wrong with him? He was thinking of his own happiness. Ella's happiness was the important thing. That and keeping her safe.

Would she be safer in Freemont, where a killer was on the loose? Or in Atlanta, far from the assailant who wanted her dead?

YOUR PARTICIPATION IS REQUESTED!

Dear Reader,

Since you are a lover of our books – we would like to get to know you!

Inside you will find a short Reader's Survey. Sharing your answers with us will help our editorial staff understand who you are and what activities you enjoy.

To thank you for your participation, we would like to send you 2 books and 2 gifts – **ABSOLUTELY FREE!**

Enjoy your gifts with our appreciation,

Pam Powers

SEE INSIDE FOR READER'S SURVEY

For Your Reading Pleasure...

YOUR READER'S SURVEY
"THANK YOU" FREE GIFTS INCLUDE:
- ▶ 2 FREE books
- ▶ 2 lovely surprise gifts

PLEASE FILL IN THE CIRCLES COMPLETELY TO RESPOND

1) What type of fiction books do you enjoy reading? (Check all that apply)
- ○ Suspense/Thrillers   ○ Action/Adventure   ○ Modern-day Romances
- ○ Historical Romance   ○ Humor   ○ Paranormal Romance

2) What attracted you most to the last fiction book you purchased on impulse?
- ○ The Title   ○ The Cover   ○ The Author   ○ The Story

3) What is usually the greatest influencer when you <u>plan</u> to buy a book?
- ○ Advertising   ○ Referral   ○ Book Review

4) How often do you access the internet?
- ○ Daily   ○ Weekly   ○ Monthly   ○ Rarely or never.

5) How many NEW paperback fiction novels have you purchased in the past 3 months?
- ○ 0 - 2   ○ 3 - 6   ○ 7 or more

YES! I have completed the Reader's Survey. Please send me the 2 FREE books and 2 FREE gifts (gifts are worth about $10) for which I qualify. I understand that I am under no obligation to purchase any books, as explained on the back of this card.

❏ I prefer the regular-print edition   ❏ I prefer the larger-print edition
153 IDL GLDH/353 IDL GLDH   107 IDL GLDH/307 IDL GLDH

FIRST NAME   LAST NAME

ADDRESS

APT.#   CITY

STATE/PROV.   ZIP/POSTAL CODE

READER SERVICE—Here's how it works:

TEN

Ella was beyond tired. Her head throbbed and every muscle in her body ached as they pulled into her driveway at the clinic.

"Are you okay?" Zach asked.

"No." She had to be truthful. "I'm tired and upset and worried about what we might find when we go inside."

"I'll check the clinic. You stay in the car."

She gave him the key and was relieved when he returned with a smile, opening the passenger door and offering her his hand.

"Everything looks just the same as when we left. Your nurse left a note. The receptionist's husband installed an alarm system. The details are on your desk."

Ella let out a grateful sigh. "That's good news."

Entering the clinic, she was overcome with relief. Not only were things back in place, but Wendy had vacuumed and mopped the floors. She'd even washed the windows, and the fresh scent of furniture polish and floor wax filled the air.

On Monday, Ella would see patients again; at least she hoped she would. No telling what the Amish families would decide after the attack. Knowing how skittish they could be, she wondered if the parents would trust their children to a doctor involved in a criminal investigation.

"Why don't you go on," she told Zach. "I need to take a nap, and there's no reason for you to stay here, especially since I have the security alarm."

"You can't get rid of me that easily." He pointed to the hallway. "Get some sleep. I'll check my email. I also need to make a few phone calls."

Although his voice was firm, she saw the concern and sincerity in his gaze.

"If you insist. But I'll set my alarm clock for an hour so I don't oversleep."

"Make that two hours, and I'll be happy."

"Can I get you something to drink before I disappear?"

"A cup of coffee would be good. Or water."

"One of each coming up."

She hurried into her kitchen and returned with coffee and a chilled bottle of water.

"The coffee's just what I need, and I'll chase it with the water. Thanks." Again, he pointed to the hallway. "Now go."

She gave him a mock salute. "Yes, sir."

He laughed, and the heaviness that had weighed her down lifted for a moment, until she entered her residence and saw a photo of Quin that sat on the hutch in her dining room. For some reason, his frown pulled her down again.

She hurried into her bedroom and locked the door—not because she was worried about Zach; she didn't fear him and believed him to be an honorable man. But she wanted to lock out the memories from her past. She had left Pennsylvania and started a new life for herself, yet no matter what she told Zach, she was vulnerable.

The security alarm would be a deterrent, but would it save her if the assailant returned? The police in Freemont were too far away to protect her. Anything could happen by the time they arrived. She wouldn't be able to summon Levi in the dead of night, since he didn't have a phone, and even if she called Zach, he lived at Fort Rickman, miles away from the Amish community.

She thought of the invitation to Atlanta. Perhaps that would offer her a reprieve, at least for a day or two. By the time she returned, the local police might have apprehended the assailant. A change of scenery could be just what she needed.

Zach would leave later today, and she'd be on her own again. He had become a comfortable—too comfortable—presence. They seemed to work well together, but he was a special agent who was merely investigating a case.

As she washed her hands and face, Ella looked into the mirror. She'd vowed never to make the mistake of getting involved with a man again. She'd done so in giving her heart to Quin, a mistake that had hurt her deeply as he became more and more reclusive and less and less interested in her.

So many times she had yearned for something more, for a family like the ones who brought their children to her Carlisle practice. She'd envied the love she'd seen reflected in the parents' eyes.

She'd had her chance and ruined it with the failure of her marriage. Again, the terrible guilt overwhelmed her. Had Quin turned away from her because she wasn't lovable, wasn't the woman he had wanted her to be? She'd made mistakes—he'd said it more than once. But did the failure of their marriage rest on her shoulders alone?

Turning away from her reflection, she dried her hands and face and then stretched across her bed, not even pulling down the Amish quilt that reminded her of the good people who put God first.

Where had she put God? He wasn't even in her life. Was that why nothing seemed to go well for her?

She gripped the edge of the quilt and closed her eyes so that everything that had happened would disappear.

So that she'd slip into oblivion, where she didn't have to worry about an evil man who had attacked her so violently he must have wanted her dead.

What was wrong with him?

Zach was sitting in Ella Jacobsen's clinic, a rural facility similar to the one where his mother had died and the very place he never wanted to be. He'd been taken in by the doctor. He needed to be a CID special agent and not the doctor's guardian, yet that's exactly what he wanted to do—protect Ella and make sure she was safe from the terrible predator.

He had never felt so committed, determined and focused on keeping someone safe, which was a good thing. But there was something else, a feeling deep in his heart that was about more than keeping a witness secure. A feeling that he couldn't explain and didn't completely understand, yet it made him stronger and tougher and more determined to do what was right.

He called Tyler Zimmerman at CID headquarters. The special agent answered on the second ring. "What's up, Zach?"

"I'm at the Children's Care Clinic and wondered if I could ask a favor."

"Shoot."

"I need a burner phone. When you head home, would you mind stopping by the PX and buying one? If you could drop it off here, that would be perfect. Otherwise I can stop by your place once you get home."

"The doc doesn't have a cell phone?"

"Negative. It's her Amish neighbor. I'm hoping he'll agree to keep the phone so Dr. Jacobsen can contact him if she's threatened in the night."

"You trust him to protect the doctor?"

"Only if someone tries to break into her clinic again.

He's the closest neighbor. The doc is taking care of his pregnant wife and will deliver their baby. That's got to have bearing on his desire to keep her safe. I'll hang out here as late as possible, but she'll eventually tell me to go home. Fort Rickman is more than a thirty-minute drive. I won't be able to respond quickly enough if someone tries to get in here."

"You know I live along Amish Road?"

"I knew you lived off post. Are you close by?"

"Just after the turnoff from town. Give her my number. In fact, I've got a spare bedroom. You're welcome to stay there."

"That sounds like a plan. How do I find your house?" Zach asked.

"You've seen the big antebellum home?"

"I have. Is that your place?"

"It belongs to Carrie York."

"Your fiancée?"

"That's right. I'm in the small ranch south of there. I'll get that phone and deliver it later today, along with a spare key to my house so you can come and go as you please."

"I appreciate the hospitality and your help. I've got a gym bag in my office and an extra set of clothing. Would you mind bringing them to me, as well?"

"Will do."

Zach felt a surge of relief. He had planned to hang out in the Amish area late into the night to make sure Ella didn't have any strange visitors. Staying at Tyler's house meant Zach could come to Ella's aid at a minute's notice.

"What about Corporal Hugh Powers?" he asked Zimmerman. "Has anything new surfaced on him?"

"I questioned him extensively, but he kept to his story. The guy's exhausted and worried to death about his wife. He seems to be the doting husband, although we both know that can be faked."

"Did he mention having PTSD?"

"Roger that. He was forthright about his condition, although he's so distraught that it's hard to say if it is caused by his deployment or by what happened to his wife."

"How's she doing?"

"Still on a ventilator and unable to talk. No one is offering any encouragement. Her kidneys started to shut down. They're watching her blood pressure and are concerned about infection."

"Have you seen her parents?"

"The dad visited early this morning. He's cranky and complains about everything that's being done. I'm giving him the benefit of the doubt and blaming it on his love for his daughter."

"Have you gotten a sense of how he and the husband get along?"

"Both men are emotional wrecks. The tension is high and one of the nurses said they've had words. I can't tell you if there's a true animosity or just the fatigue and worry that comes when a loved one is in critical condition."

Zach looked at his watch. "Let me know if anything new surfaces."

"Will do. I'll be in touch."

After disconnecting, Zach called Sergeant Abrams. "Any success with Daniel Fisher?"

"He's a strange one. I'm not sure if he's really Amish or just pretending to be in the fold to keep his father happy. We're running a ballistics on the rifle. Seems a coincidence that both he and Levi Miller own the same type of gun."

"Actually, it makes sense. The Model 94 is a good hunting rifle. Perfect for deer or wild boar, and it's a dependable weapon, yet fairly inexpensive. The Amish use their rifles to hunt for food. Seems the 94 would be a good choice."

"You might be right."

"Did you question Daniel about his past relationship with Mary Kate?"

"He says he knew who she was and that's it. Do you think he was jealous of Levi?"

"It's a possibility. Or he could be a protective older brother who's concerned about his sister's marriage. He comes back to Georgia on the pretense of helping his dad. Maybe he saw Levi and Mary Kate together. Her father said Levi had been hanging around. Of course, Levi's story is that he was inquiring about the twins. His wife is pregnant, and they're worried the condition the twins have could be passed to their own baby."

Abrams picked up on the direction Zach was headed. "So Daniel sees Levi with Mary Kate and suspects his brother-in-law might be involved with her again?"

"Stranger things have happened. Lots of folks jump to the wrong conclusion. Daniel seems to be a bit on the hot-headed side. I can see him getting aggravated and feeling that he needs to defend his sister's name."

"So he tries to kill Mary Kate?" Abrams asked.

"He could have followed her to the clinic. The storm works into his plans. He cuts the electricity, hoping the doc will think it's an area-wide power outage. She leaves the house to tend to the generator, and he confronts the twins' mother. Maybe he wanted to scare her or threaten her, and everything goes south. Emotions could have run wild. He fires without thinking through his actions."

The officer let out a stiff breath. "I see what you mean. We'll hold him for another hour or so and see if his story changes. Something needs to break soon."

"We've got bits of information. Somehow they have to fit together. Stay in touch."

After Zach disconnected, he called CID headquarters. Sergeant Raynard Otis answered.

"Hey, Ray, it's Special Agent Swain. I'm interested in talking to law enforcement in Alabama that would have jurisdiction over an Amish community. As I recall, it's located not far from the town of Harmony."

"Yes, sir. You've got that right. Special Agent Colby Voss was involved in a case near there. Give me a minute and I'll access the information."

Zach stretched back in the chair and waited. His eyes wandered to the picture of Quin Jacobsen on a table behind Ella's desk. He needed to find more information about her husband's death.

Ray came back on the line. "I found it, sir." He provided the name and phone number of the lead officer. "Sheriff Lewis Stone should be able to help you."

"Thanks, Ray. I've got another request. A research physician died in Memphis about eight months ago. He was attending a medical conference and drove his rental car to one of the bridges that span the Mississippi River. Supposedly, he jumped, and his body washed up on shore some days later. I want to contact the law enforcement agency that handled the case."

"Do you have more information, sir?"

"Only the doctor's name. Quin—or Quinton—Jacobsen. He lived in Carlisle, Pennsylvania, and worked for a Harrisburg research center that studied genetic diseases affecting children, primarily Amish children." Zach hurried to Ella's desk and leaned over the invitation he'd seen the night before. "The name of the facility is the Harrisburg Genetic Research Center."

"I'll do some checking and get back to you."

After disconnecting, Zach called the Alabama sheriff. He introduced himself and stated the information he needed. "Do you know a Daniel Fisher? He supposedly has lived in an Amish community near you. Medium height. Kind of bulky build. Probably five-eleven and two hundred pounds. No distinguishing features or marks that I was able to see. His sister may live nearby, although I don't have a name for her."

"I know Fisher," the chief quickly replied. "He built a little house on the edge of the Amish community. Far as we could determine, he wasn't living the Amish life. He'd come into town at times and do some odd jobs to make money. At first, he seemed like a hard worker, but the longer he stayed on a job, the lazier he became. A number of times he argued over the pay he received, declaring that he'd been promised a higher wage. I've known some of the construction bosses who hired him. They're God-fearing men who are known for their honesty and the care they provide their workers. I trust them and their business practices. A couple of the firms fired Fisher after he put up a fuss."

"Were other Amish men working construction?"

"A few do at times, especially when money is tight. Farming is hard work. In the lean years, when crops don't do well, we see a number of Amish lads looking for employment to support their families. A couple guys work as volunteer firemen. They get paid when they go out on a call. The Amish ladies sell their produce and baked goods at our Saturday farmers' market. Some of them take in sewing and alterations."

"But Fisher didn't seem like part of the Amish community?"

"That was the way I saw it. He was standoffish and could be surly at times, which, as you probably know, doesn't fit the Amish mold."

"Did you ever suspect him of illegal activity?"

The chief hesitated a moment and then pulled in a deep breath. "Funny you should mention it. We had some petty thefts in the local area. Not big-ticket items, but small things that could be easily pawned in one of the neighboring towns. A few GPS systems were lifted from un-locked cars. A woman's purse was taken when she was in the gym. We later found her wallet and handbag in a city trash can. The credit cards hadn't been used, but two hundred dollars in cash was gone."

"Did you suspect Fisher?"

"He was seen in town that day. I didn't have any wit-nesses or evidence, but it made me wonder. I talked to him about where he'd been and listened as he provided a lame excuse about walking to town on a back road. Seemed suspicious to me, but I never found anything that tied him to the robberies."

"Did he mention his father or sister or an English woman named Mary Kate Powers, all of whom are from Freemont, Georgia?"

"Not that I recall, but he does have a sister in this area. Elizabeth Glick. She and her husband are good people. If only Daniel had taken after them."

Zach disconnected with a nervous feeling in his gut. Fisher didn't fit the Amish mold, yet would he have bro-ken into the clinic and attacked two women in cold blood? Something didn't add up.

Resting his head back in the chair, Zach closed his eyes and let his thoughts wander. Sometimes when he was stuck on a case, if he gave his mind free rein the answer would come like a flash. Today, all he got was confusion.

His cell rang. He checked the monitor before he con-nected and greeted Sergeant Otis. "Hey, Ray. Thanks for getting back to me."

"I've got contact info for the Memphis agency that han-dled the death investigation for Quinton Jacobsen." The sergeant provided a name and the police department's phone number.

"Good work, Ray. I owe you."

"Negative, sir. Just doing my job."

Zach smiled as he clicked off. Ray was a good man and an asset to the CID.

After tapping in the phone number he had provided, Zach pulled out his notebook and made a notation of Officer George Davis's name and number.

A receptionist answered and redirected him to Davis's private line. Zach groaned when the call went to voice mail. He left an overview of the information he needed, along with the call-back details.

"I'd appreciate any help you could provide," Zach added before he clicked off.

He spent the next thirty minutes checking emails on his phone. Hearing a car turn into the clinic driveway, he peered through the window and then hurried outside to meet Tyler.

"Thanks, buddy." Zach took the clothing and burner phone. "You're fast and reliable."

"Turns out we had an extra phone in the office that we didn't use on a previous case. That meant I didn't have to stop at the PX." Tyler handed him a key. "This is to the front door of my place. I need to run a few errands in town. See you whenever."

Zach slipped the key into his pocket and placed the gym bag and extra clothing in his own car as Tyler headed back to Freemont.

Seeing Levi on his front porch, Zach hurried to talk to the Amish man about keeping the phone as security for Ella. Thankfully, he agreed, and after giving Levi a short course in cell phone usage, Zach returned to the clinic.

He downed the last of the water and settled onto the couch with a sigh, realizing how tired he felt. He'd gone too many hours without any shut-eye.

After stretching out his legs and leaning his head back, Zach closed his eyes and drifted into a light sleep.

Visions swirled through his slumber. He saw Ella lying

on the floor of her clinic, bleeding from a gunshot wound. Another doctor leaned over her, doing CPR. Zach rushed to her side, but hands held him back. He fought off their grasp and screamed for someone to save her. But when the doctor stepped away, Zach could see her face. It wasn't Ella, but his mother.

He jerked awake and sat up, unaware of where he was for half a second until he got his bearings.

His cell phone rang. Reaching for it, he connected to the call and listened as the Memphis cop identified himself.

"I pulled the file on the case to be sure my information was correct," the officer went on. "Mr. Jacobsen attended the seminar held at Saint Jude's Medical Center. He stayed at the Peabody Hotel downtown. When we traced his steps the night he disappeared, he had gone out to dinner with colleagues and had returned to the hotel, claiming he was tired."

Zach pulled out his notebook and pen and jotted down some of the facts.

"At approximately 8:00 p.m.," the cop continued, "Dr. Jacobsen changed his return ticket for a flight later that night and checked out of his hotel. Security cameras spotted his car heading on I-55 over the Memphis-Arkansas Memorial Bridge forty minutes later. He parked the rental on the far side of the river. Sometime that night, he must have hurled himself into the water."

"Who alerted you to his disappearance?"

"Dr. Ian Webb. He was Jacobsen's assistant. Webb tried to contact Jacobsen the next morning to verify the time they would drive to the airport together. When Jacobsen didn't answer, Webb became worried. He talked to the front desk and was even more concerned when he learned the researcher had checked out of the hotel the night prior. Webb called Jacobsen's wife. She hadn't heard from her husband. We found the abandoned rental car later that day. Search teams scoured the banks of the Mississippi, hoping to uncover some sign of the missing man. The following day, a couple of fishermen found him tangled in some debris along the shore. We notified the wife, but she was already en route to Memphis."

"Dr. Ella Jacobsen flew to Memphis?"

"No, sir. She drove."

Zach let out a stiff breath. "That's got to be a two-day trip. Probably more than nine hundred miles."

"She insisted her husband would never take his own life, but we hear that a lot. I'm sure you do, as well. Mrs. Jacobsen was adamant that he hadn't taken his life and became openly hostile at our attempts to help."

"Did she provide an explanation for her antagonism?"

"She kept saying her husband was working on a cure for a new disease and focused on helping children who suffered from the disability. She couldn't believe that he would have jumped from the bridge. He was afraid of water and didn't know how to swim. As I recall, she couldn't, either. She said he never would have chosen that type of death. Bottom line, she refused to accept our findings and became somewhat belligerent, so much so that we had to warn her to control her outbursts."

"How'd that go over?"

"Not well. She stormed out of my office and said she refused to accept suicide as the cause of death."

"Have you heard from her since?"

"Not after the body was released. She had him buried in Pennsylvania, then sold her house in Carlisle and moved South. We told her to keep in contact, but she failed to do so. Glad someone else is looking into the death. For some reason, I haven't been able to get the case off my mind." The cop sighed. "It might sound strange, but I keep wondering if she knew more than she was willing to reveal."

Before Zach could comment, the door from the hallway

opened and Ella stepped into the waiting room, wearing a broad smile and a fresh outfit. Her hair was damp, indicating she had probably showered.

Zach hadn't figured her for being a suspect. Had he been too focused on her pretty face to think of her as anything but an innocent bystander?

"She's in the middle of it, I feel sure," the officer stated before he disconnected.

As much as Zach wanted to ignore the last phone call, he had to use caution. The Memphis police considered Ella a person of interest. What was wrong with him? He'd never been suspicious of her. Was he losing the investigative skills he needed to find the assailant before he struck again?

Levi Miller, Hugh Powers, Daniel Fisher and even Bob Landers could be involved in some way. What about Ella? Could she be involved, as well?

ELEVEN

Trouble. The look in Zach's eyes told Ella something was wrong. Terribly wrong.

"Did you get bad news?" she asked, almost afraid to learn what was causing his sour expression.

Earlier he had been concerned about her well-being and had insisted she rest. Now, his face was filled with questions and suspicion.

"Just tracking down some information."

"About Daniel Fisher?" she asked.

"The Freemont police are questioning him."

She glanced out the window to the Miller house. "I hope that doesn't cause Sarah more upset."

When Zach didn't answer, Ella took a step closer. "I'm fixing something to eat. You must be hungry."

"Anything would be appreciated." He got up and started to walk away.

She grabbed his arm. "Look, I don't know who you were talking to on the phone, but something's going on, and I have a feeling it involves me. Why don't you just come out with whatever is bothering you?"

He stared at her for a moment and then nodded. "You're right. It involves you and your husband. I contacted the Memphis police who handled the investigation of his death. They said you drove there, and you were adamant that your husband couldn't have taken his life."

"And that bothers you because I stood up for my husband?"

"What do you know that you weren't willing to tell them?" Zach demanded.

"I know how my husband reacted to stress. He became more committed to finding answers. That was the type of person he was. I've never seen him morose or despondent."

"I thought you said he wasn't acting like himself."

"He was upset about the data that was collected on the children he had treated. There was something about three sets of twins. I told you that. They didn't respond like the other children. That's why I called the research center in Harrisburg when I first suspected that Shelly and Stacey had CED. I wanted to make sure the protocol hadn't changed and that the treatment was the same as Quin had determined more than a year ago."

"If your husband was upset about the findings, he may have blamed himself. Did the twins get worse? Did any children succumb to the disease?"

She shook her head. "No, it was nothing like that. No one died. All the children were treated and survived."

"Then what was the problem?"

"I don't know. I'm not sure he even knew. But something was amiss."

"And that something—whatever it was—could have been too much for him to handle. Sounds as if your husband was temperamental."

"Aren't all geniuses that way?"

"So he was a genius?"

"He was an intelligent man who had a love of science and research. He understood genetics and how recessive genes manifest in small, limited populations. It was his life's work."

"That led to his death."

"He didn't take his own life," Ella insisted.

"You think someone killed him."

She gasped. "I never said that."

"What else could it be? If he didn't jump of his own volition, then someone pushed him. That's a crime, Ella. It's called murder."

"He could have slipped and fallen," she suggested.

"Did you see the bridge? Is that likely?"

She shook her head, realizing Zach was right. Quin didn't lose his footing and slip off the bridge. Nor had he jumped. He was afraid of water and had never learned to swim. There were other ways that would have been less traumatic to end his life, but again, that wasn't Quin.

She looked at Zach and saw the questions in his eyes. What was he keeping from her?

"Did you drive to Memphis or were you already there?" he asked, his voice stern.

"What?"

"It's evident by your facial expression when you talk about your husband that something was amiss in your marriage. You wanted to fix everything, but you couldn't. Would it be better to have your husband die rather than face what was to come? Had he asked for a divorce? Was there insurance? You could have built an even larger clinic if he had a big policy, but that money wouldn't be paid if it was suicide. You didn't think about that, did you, Ella?"

Tears filled her eyes, and she fought to keep them in check. "I can't believe you would suspect me." She pointed to the door. "I'd appreciate you leaving now."

His face changed again. "I'm not leaving. You need protection. I had to find out if there could be any hint of truth to what the Memphis officer shared."

"You were testing me?" Her anger increased. Today

of all days, she didn't need more hassle. "I thought you were on my side."

"I had to be sure which side you were on, Ella."

"Right now, I'm frustrated and angry. Stay in the waiting room, if you want, but I'm going back to my residence."

"I had to make sure, Ella, that you were innocent of any wrongdoing."

"And when will you need to make sure again, Zach? I can't handle someone who doesn't believe in me and changes in a heartbeat. I thought I could trust you. Now I realize I can't."

She turned and hurried from the room overcome with emotion, from upset and heartache to a feeling of being abandoned and wrongly accused. Shame on Zach for playing tricks on her. Shame on her for believing he was something other than an investigator focused on the case. She had learned her lesson, and she wouldn't make the same mistake again.

Zach wished he could take back the callous comments he'd made. Too many investigations and too many cross-examinations had made him aggressive. He walked down the hallway and knocked on the closed kitchen door. Would Ella hear him, and if she did hear his knock, would she want to talk to him? He doubted he would be welcome, but he needed to tell her what had happened.

Again, he rapped on the door.

Footsteps sounded, and it cracked open. She stood on the threshold with one hand on the door and the other on her hip. Her gaze was guarded.

"I'm sorry," he said. "I was acting like an overzealous investigator. You don't understand, I'm sure, but law enforcers need to be careful and get to the bottom of every situation."

"You believed the Memphis police officer instead of believing me."

"I was wrong, Ella. I'm sorry if my questions upset you."

"It wasn't your questions as much as the hostility I heard in your voice. You suspected me. You probably still do."

He couldn't say anything to change her mind, he felt sure. Maybe with time she'd start to trust him again.

"I need to bring you up-to-date." He took a step closer. "Then I'll leave."

Did he detect surprise in her expression? Had she thought he'd stand guard through the night, when she had been so insistent about wanting him to leave?

"Special Agent Tyler Zimmerman stopped by the clinic with a cell phone. I gave it to Levi Miller. Here's the number." Zach handed her a small card. "Program it into your phone. Levi will be next door and will respond immediately if you feel threatened or hear anything or anyone outside."

"Are you sure Levi doesn't mind?"

"He's more than happy to help out."

"Then you think he's trustworthy?" Her question held more than a touch of irony.

"Tyler lives along Amish Road. You've probably seen the antebellum home."

"He lives there?"

Zach smiled. "He's engaged to the woman who inherited the big house from her father. Tyler lives in the brick ranch south of it."

"I know the Amish neighbors on the other side of the old home. Isaac and Ruth Lapp have brought their young son, Joseph, to the clinic," Ella murmured.

"Tyler invited me to stay at his place for the next couple of days. I won't be far. Call me if you have a problem."

"But you live on post."

"I do, in the bachelor officers' quarters, but the drive takes a bit of time. I wanted to be closer to you."

She leaned against the doorjamb. "Thank you, Zach."

"Cops have to worse-case every situation, Ella. It's not personal. It's the way we roll. I don't disbelieve you. I just needed to make sure. Your reaction proved to me that you've been truthful and sincere."

"Evidently I don't understand law enforcement."

He almost smiled. "And I don't understand medicine. Doctors have never been on my list of most favorite people."

"Is it personal?"

He pursed his lips. "I'm not sure what you mean."

"Personal, as in a female doc broke your heart so you won't like any of us."

"No girlfriend. No fiancée. No ex-wife."

"Then I'm wrong."

"It stems from my childhood, but I'll leave it at that."

"And did that play in to your verbal attack against me?" she asked.

"It wasn't an attack, Ella. I had questions that needed to be answered."

"Which seemed more like an interrogation."

He nodded. "I understand how you could misinterpret my intentions."

She looked into the kitchen. "I've got a pot of chili cooking, if you're hungry."

"Are you sure you want company?"

"Of course. I'm sorry if I came off as antagonistic."

Zach smiled. "Isn't that what you accused me of being?"

"And you were exactly that, but I'm tired and not as forgiving as I should be."

He raised his eyebrow. "Did I ask for forgiveness?"

She stared at him for a long moment. "If you didn't, you should have. I'm trying to play nice."

"You're succeeding."

"Does that mean you'll accept my invitation to dinner?"

"Most assuredly. As they say in the South, 'My mama didn't raise no fools.' I'd enjoy sharing a meal with you, but only if you let me take you out sometime."

He hadn't expected Ella's surprised expression.

"Are you asking me out on a date?" she asked.

"No." He raised his hand as if to block anything she had been thinking along those lines. "A friendly dinner to pay you back for your hospitality."

She blushed. "Now I'm feeling embarrassed. I wasn't fishing for a date. You took me by surprise, especially after I kicked you out."

"You made chili."

"I'm reheating chili that was already made," she corrected.

"That makes no difference. Food is food, and I'm hungry."

Ella smiled. "The way I figure it, you've got to be down a couple meals."

"It's par for the course for a special agent. We work 24/7 when needed. I can live on coffee for longer than you would like to know."

"Has your doctor mentioned the damage that could do to your stomach and esophagus? You're opening yourself up to acid reflux and even more serious complications."

Again, he held up his hand. "I'm doing okay, and I don't have a primary care doc. If I get sick—and it's rare that I do—I go on sick call. Although I can't remember the last time I needed to be treated."

"Hardy stock, eh?"

"Maybe it's the coffee." Zach couldn't help but smile.

Ella laughed. The tension that he'd felt earlier evaporated. She stepped away from the door and motioned him into the kitchen.

"We'll eat in here, if you don't mind."

He glanced at the vase of flowers by the window. "The least I can do is set the table."

She pointed to a cabinet near the sink. "You'll find silverware in the top drawer. We'll need soup spoons, as well as knives and forks."

Ella shoved a cast-iron skillet into the oven. "Do you like corn bread?"

"I do. That's good Georgia food."

"It'll be done by the time the chili is hot. There's butter in the refrigerator, if you want to put it on the table while I make a salad."

She also made a pitcher of sweet tea.

Seeing the sugar she dumped into the warm liquid, Zach had to laugh. "You're from up north, yet you make tea like a Southerner?"

"Does that seem strange?" She smiled. "Adding sugar when the tea is warm ensures it will dissolve, which is a lot more economical than putting it in individual glasses. Plus I like the taste."

"No wonder the locals enjoy having you around."

"Only some of them," she said as she dropped ice into the pitcher.

"You've had problems before?"

"Not really. It's just that some folks, especially the older Amish, don't want me interfering in their lives."

"Is that what they've said?"

She nodded. "A few, mainly men. The woman are relieved to have a doctor nearby in case their children get sick."

Zach glanced out the window. "Do you ever get lonely out here, all by yourself?"

She hesitated for a moment before she pulled two

glasses from the cabinet. "The weekends can be long, although I usually have something that needs attention around the clinic."

She filled the glasses before glancing up at him. "What about you? Don't you ever get lonely?"

"I wouldn't call it lonely. Usually I stay busy. If I have some downtime, I head to the gym or go for a jog outside."

"You can't jog all day long."

He laughed. "You're right. After jogging, I shower and leave my BOQ, seeking food. Like a hunter of old, only I don't have to stalk my prey. It's usually served at one of the local restaurants. Which," he said with a smile, "brings us back to my earlier question. Would you like to join me for a meal sometime?" He shrugged. "We can call it a business dinner if we talk about the investigation. If we stick to more general topics, it can be a chance for two people who know each other to connect. Or—" he smiled "—if you'd feel better, we could call it a date."

Ella laughed. Her face softened, her eyes sparkled in spite of being tired, and she took on a new lighthearted appearance that he found enchanting. A date would be fun.

"Is this your normal modus operandi?" she asked.

"You speak Latin?"

She nodded. "Most doctors have a good understanding of the language."

"I took it in high school," he admitted.

"Really?" She seemed surprised.

"My mother loved biblical Roman times. She died when I was young. Reading the books she treasured and learning the language she had studied allowed me to feel closer to her."

"I'm sorry."

Zach shrugged. "We all carry baggage, the hurts and struggles from the past."

Ella nodded knowingly. "Would I be correct in assuming that your mother's death has something to do with your dislike of the medical profession?"

Not only did the doctor like to talk, she was also perceptive.

"I thought we were discussing dinner together."

She nodded again and turned to ladle the chili into soup bowls. "That's exactly what we were talking about. Mind if I ask one more question."

No telling where she was headed. "Shoot."

"Do you invite all the witnesses in your investigations to dine with you?"

Ella stood at the stove with her back to him, so he couldn't read her expression. Was she still being frivolous and lighthearted, or had the mention of his mother's death turned her more pensive?

Zach regretted the direction their conversation had gone. "Perhaps dinner should wait until the investigation is over."

Which made a whole lot more sense than going out when the case was still active. Either way, she was right to have asked the question. Zach didn't usually socialize with witnesses. Make that never. He had never before gone out with a witness.

So what made Ella different?

Turning with a hot soup bowl in hand, she stared at him for half a second before placing the dish on the table.

Her pretty face and blue eyes looked as perplexed as he felt. Talk about a flood of emotion. Zach prided himself on being a man of action, on not letting his personal life get in the way of anything to do with his job. Yet he'd done exactly that, no matter how much he wanted to think being with Ella wasn't personal.

He glanced at the chili she'd set before him and inhaled the rich aroma. "This smells and looks delicious.

For me, chili usually comes out of a can. This has home-made written all over it."

She smiled and turned back to the stove for her own bowl. "You asked what I do on weekends. Often I cook and then freeze what I fix in smaller containers. That way if I'm busy with patients late into the day, I can eat a nourishing dinner without having to spend time getting everything made."

"Smart lady."

She turned back and smiled. "You're an affirming person."

He rounded the table and helped her with her chair. "And you're perceptive," he said.

"Which a doctor needs to be."

Settling into his seat, Zach thought about what she'd said. "My father was a positive man. Perhaps I learned affirmation from him."

She nodded. "He was probably worried about you after your mother died. Sounds like he was a good man who wanted to build up his young son."

"He *was* a good man. I lost him last year. Too young."

"Do you have other family?" Ella asked.

Zach shook his head. "What about you?"

"An only child. My father's still alive, but we don't have much of a relationship. I call him at Christmas. He sends a check for my birthday."

She glanced down. "The chili's getting cold."

Zach nodded and reached for his spoon, then noticed that she had bowed her head as if offering a blessing.

When she glanced up, he smiled sheepishly. "I haven't paused to give thanks before eating since I was a kid. My mother always led us in saying grace before meals. You've taken me back."

Ella's expression lightened again and the sparkle returned to her eyes. "The Amish are rubbing off on me. I'm not religious, and I haven't had much to do with God for years, but their trust in the Lord and the comments they mention about doing His will have made me think about the importance of faith. For your information, research has proved that people of faith have a better chance of surviving a significant illness, such as cancer, than unbelievers."

He raised the soup spoon. "So you're experimenting on yourself?"

"I hadn't thought about it in that way. If faith has a positive influence on quality of life, then shouldn't I attempt to integrate it into my own?"

She sounded clinical.

"Doc, you're talking with your head instead of your heart." Zach tasted the chili. "My compliments to the chef."

"Thanks. My mother worked. I took over the kitchen at a younger age than most of my peers. Cooking was something I could do right."

He glanced at her as he enjoyed another spoonful of her chili. He might not be as perceptive as the doc, but he sensed she came with some baggage, too.

Zach thought of his own past and the pain he still carried. Pain and guilt. Not that he had to go there, especially not tonight. He needed to turn the discussion to mundane matters of little consequence, instead of faith and lonely children who couldn't find their way.

The conversation changed to lighthearted chatter that Zach enjoyed. How long had it been since he'd relaxed with a woman? Most of the ones he associated with were army types who talked about military topics, like the guys.

The doc wasn't one of the guys, at least not tonight. Maybe in medical circles, when she was spouting facts about the pediatric needs of children, she might seem more focused on her career. Right now, sitting in her warm and welcoming kitchen, eating the hearty chili she had made, took him away from the investigation that had brought them together.

After coffee and a slice of apple pie that Levi's wife had sent home with them, Zach looked at his watch and scooted back from the table.

"I don't want to overstay my welcome." He carried his soup bowl and silverware to the sink. "Let me do the dishes while you put the leftover chili away."

"You know how to get on a woman's good side." Ella smiled as she placed her own bowl in the sink. "Just rinse the dishes, and I'll get to them later."

"No, ma'am. I'm not leaving you with dishes to wash." He ran water in the sink and added soap. "I'll have these done in a flash."

"You could use the dishwasher."

He nodded. "I could, but you'll think more of me if I wash them by hand, then dry them and put them away. You're exhausted and need a full night's sleep, instead of spending time tidying up the kitchen."

"I won't argue with your logic, Mr. Swain." She pulled a container from an overhead cabinet, transferred the rest of the chili and placed it in the refrigerator. "There's enough left over for lunch, if you're in the neighborhood."

The invitation warmed his heart. Zach quickly washed and rinsed the dishes and then dried them and handed them to Ella, who put them in the proper places on the shelves.

Once that was done he wiped his hands on a dish towel. "Thanks for the chili and for the opportunity to relax a bit."

"I enjoyed it, too."

"You've got the number to my cell?"

She nodded. "It's programmed into my phone. I've also got the number to contact Levi. Hopefully, I won't need to call either of you."

"I'll go out through the clinic."

He held the hallway door open, and she walked ahead of him. Returning to the scene of the attack brought them back to the reality of what had happened, and the levity Zach had felt in her kitchen came to an abrupt end.

Ella hesitated when they reached the waiting room. "I haven't adequately thanked you, Zach, for taking me to the hospital. You stayed throughout the night. That meant a lot to me, and I know hospitals aren't your favorite places to be."

"That's your perceptive nature. I hope I didn't embarrass you when I quizzed the nurse about why the lab and X-ray results were taking so long."

"I appreciated having a champion." She placed her hand on his arm. Her touch was light, yet it had an effect on him. He stepped closer, seeing the openness of her gaze, the fullness of her lips. She leaned closer and for a moment he longed to touch his lips to hers.

Intellectually, he knew how foolish his reactions seemed, yet he couldn't find the wherewithal to step away. Some unknown yet attractive force pulled him to her.

"You're a good man, Zach." Her voice was low and rich with resonance, as if she meant to say much more than the words themselves.

His chest swelled, and he felt taller and stronger and ready to slay giants or dragons or anything untoward that might come against her. For a moment, he was her champion, a man who would protect her from harm, who would give her his allegiance and—did he dare acknowledge an even deeper feeling?—give her his heart.

The office phone rang.

Ella blinked, as if some imaginary thread held them together and she wasn't ready to cut free from its hold.

"I need to go," Zach said, coming to his senses much

too quickly. The world seemed to spin around him as he turned and headed for the door.

The phone continued to ring, but when he looked back, she remained in the middle of her office, staring in his direction, oblivious to the phone or anything else except him.

TWELVE

Ella couldn't move. Her heart thumped hard and a knot had formed in her throat. Not from tears. She'd cried too many times after Quin had died, and she didn't know how to rebuild her life.

The lump in her throat tonight was pure emotion that made her want to wrap her arms around the handsome special agent's shoulders and have him pull her into his embrace, as he'd done yesterday in the hallway when she'd remembered the gun.

The gun?

All too clearly, she saw the glaring light that had almost blinded her and the assailant's hand holding the revolver.

Earlier, as she sat in the kitchen with Zach, Ella had pushed everything that had happened the night before out of her mind. Now it flooded over her. Mary Kate's scream, the pounding rain, her own attempt to come to the young mother's rescue, only to find a man, bathed in shadow, standing at her desk.

She turned, seeing the desk again.

And heard the phone.

How long had it been ringing?

Tripping over herself, she raced to her desk and lifted the handset to her ear.

A dial tone sounded.

She tapped in star 69 to recapture the caller's number. A number she recognized. Nancy Vaughn, director of the Harrisburg Genetic Research Center.

Pulling in a deep breath to calm her pounding heart, Ella tugged on the curtain and watched through the window as Zach drove out onto the main road. She stared after him as his taillights disappeared into the night.

A sense of sadness washed over her, bringing with it a nervous anxiety that made her scurry to the front door of her clinic. She checked the lock and engaged the dead bolt, refusing to dwell on what could happen if the locks didn't hold. Stepping back into her office, she checked the side door to her clinic, then the kitchen and main doors to her house.

Satisfied with the extra protection the dead bolts provided, Ella returned to her office and called the director.

"I thought something might have happened when you didn't answer," the woman said, sounding breathless. "I was worried about you."

Ella tried to laugh off her concern. "I was in the other room."

"You were going through Quin's things?"

"No, why would you think that?" she asked.

"One of the times we talked, you mentioned that you still had boxes from his office to unpack."

"You're right, but that wasn't what I was doing." Ella rubbed her free hand over her face. The spot where she'd been struck was tender to the touch. "I'm returning your call, Dr. Vaughn. Was there something you needed?"

"It's time to stop with the formality. I'm Nancy, and I called to let you know that I reserved a room for you at the hotel. Even if you can't make the afternoon symposium, be sure to join us at the benefit that evening. It's what Quin would want."

Quin had never been a black-tie type of guy. In fact, Ella had had to convince him to wear a suit to their wedding.

"I appreciate the offer, Nancy, but I just don't think—"

"Let's talk in the morning. Sometimes things look brighter in the light of day."

But this had nothing to do with daylight or sunshine.

"Have you heard from Ross Underwood recently?" the director asked. "He was extremely distraught when Quin died. I know the two men were close."

"Ross called soon after I opened the Children's Care Clinic and asked if there was anything I needed. I appreciated his thoughtfulness."

"He was worried about you, Ella. We all were. As I mentioned at Quin's funeral, I would have liked you to join the team."

"Research isn't my interest, Nancy, but I was grateful for the offer. Quin's work was the main focus of his life. He felt strongly about the good that was being done, especially with the Amish Project."

"We share those feelings, of course. I won't keep you tonight, but I'm counting on you to join us on Friday. I'll be in touch."

Ella stared at the invitation after she disconnected, feeling even more confused. Over the last twenty-four hours, she had experienced a gamut of emotions. Everything from grief for Quin to a surprising attraction for another man.

She flipped off the light and returned to the kitchen, locking the door to the hallway behind her. Peering out of the side window, she was relieved to see a faint glow coming from the Miller home.

Sarah and Levi were probably sitting in their kitchen, the room lit by a gaslight.

Her cell rang.

Surprised, she smiled when she saw Zach's name on the monitor. "I hope nothing is wrong," she said in greeting.

"I'm at Special Agent Zimmerman's house. Just wanted to let you know that I'm not far away. Don't hesitate to call me."

A warmth filled her chest. "You're being cautious, which I appreciate. The assailant was probably after meds. Nonmedical folks think that doctors stockpile drugs. That's why he came back today."

"Let's hope that's what he was looking for. Did you set your security alarm?"

"Not yet, but I will."

"Don't hesitate to call me," Zach repeated.

She disconnected, armed the security alarm and walked into her bedroom. Knowing he was close by was reassuring. The assailant wouldn't come back. At least not tonight. She'd sleep soundly and wake refreshed in the morning.

Peering out the rear window into the darkness, she felt a ripple of anxiety stir within her.

At least she hoped she would be able to sleep.

Zach hadn't planned to call. He had said goodbye to Ella less than five minutes earlier, yet as he'd pulled into Tyler's driveway, he was tapping the call prompt and raising the phone to his ear.

Was it important for Ella to know he wasn't far away, or was it important for him to hear her voice again? Either way, the call hadn't been necessary, although he had heard concern in her voice when she asked if anything was wrong. Nothing was wrong on his end, and in a way, everything seemed right. Except that was glossing over a very real problem about an attack against two women and an assailant still on the loose.

Zach stepped from his car and grabbed his gym bag

and extra clothing. The spare outfits would get him to the weekend. Perhaps the investigation would be solved by then.

Tyler opened the front door before Zach could pull the house key from his pocket. "Welcome to rural life." He motioned Zach inside. "I picked up pizza on the way home, by the way. I wasn't sure when you'd get here."

"Thanks, buddy, but I ate at Ella's."

Tyler smirked with surprise. "Since when did Dr. Jacobsen become Ella?"

"You know her?"

"I know of her, and it's all good. She's treated my neighbors' son, and they give her high praise."

"We spent a number of hours together at the ER last night," Zach explained, "while waiting for her test results."

"I've heard some recent complaints about the local hospital."

"If what we experienced is any indication of their competence..." Zach shrugged. "But then, I've never been a fan of anything medical. In all fairness, the nurse and the doctor said they were short staffed."

Tyler pointed to the hallway. "Guest room is on the left. The bathroom is to the right. The coffeepot is programmed for 6:00 a.m., if that works for you."

"Sounds good."

"Colas are in the fridge, or I can brew a pot of decaf."

Zach held up his hand. "Thanks, but I need to hit the sack."

"I'm right behind you," Tyler said. "Tomorrow afternoon, the chief is headed to Fort Belvoir. He assigned me to go with him. It's last minute, but that's typical."

"Have a safe trip."

"Will do, but I'll see you in the morning."

Once in the bedroom, Zach placed his cell on the nightstand and checked the volume. If Ella phoned, he wanted to be sure to hear the call.

If only he had met her before the assailant broke into her clinic. Then he could have invited her out to dinner and they could have called it a date.

He would have liked that.

His eyelids grew heavy. The last things he thought about were Ella's blue eyes and the way her laughter touched a lonely portion of his heart.

THIRTEEN

The night had never seemed so dark, nor had Ella been so aware of sounds. She heard the throaty croak of bullfrogs and the incessant chirp of cicadas, but other noises—a tree branch brushing against the house, a groan as the hardwood floors settled, the heat turning on and the freezer emptying a tray of ice cubes into the holding container—seemed especially annoying tonight. Even the *ticktock* of her alarm clock grated on her nerves.

She draped one arm over her eyes in an attempt to blot out the world, but tired as she was, she couldn't sleep. With a frustrated sign, she flipped onto her side, buried her head in the pillow and, at some point, drifted off.

In the middle of the night, her eyes blinked open. She glanced at the clock on her nightstand: 2:00 a.m.

What had awakened her?

Ella raised up and listened, unable to decipher a sound that came from the side of the house.

A scratching. Surely not a rodent?

She stepped from her bed and grabbed her robe off the nearby chair. Slipping into the thick flannel, she toed on her slippers and pulled back the curtain ever so slightly. Peering outside, she couldn't identify anything, yet the sound continued. She grabbed her cell off the nightstand

and stepped into the living area, where she stopped again and listened.

The noise sounded like a chisel, biting into wood.

Her kitchen door!

Before she could hit the prompt to call Levi, the back door opened. Fear swept over her. Seconds later, the security alarm blared a warning.

The sound filled the house.

Heart pounding, Ella ran back to her bedroom and hesitated. The assailant would expect to find her there, so she scurried across the hall to the guest room, closed and locked the door and entered the attached bath, grateful for the night light that illuminated the room ever so slightly. She shut the bathroom door and turned the lock, but felt little sense of protection.

With trembling hands, she tapped Levi's number. Voice mail.

What had happened? He knew she was alone.

A swell of panic filled her chest. Had Levi ignored her call for help because he was in her house? Footsteps sounded. She backed up against the bathroom door.

Not Levi. It couldn't be Levi.

She fumbled with her phone. It slipped through her fingers. She caught it in midair, her heart in her throat.

Hitting speed dial, she called Zach.

The phone rang in her ear. Why didn't he pick up?

The assailant broke through the locked guest room door.

Oh, God, she silently prayed.

"Ella?" Zach's voice.

The security alarm continued to scream. She pushed the phone closer to her ear. "He's in the bedroom."

"I'm on the way. Gouge out his eyes, jam your hand up under his chin, knee him where it hurts."

Inwardly, she screamed for Zach to hurry. She didn't have time for lessons on self-defense.

Heavy footsteps crossed the bedroom.

She glanced down as the doorknob jiggled.

"I know you're in there." A gruff voice, muffled as if he was speaking through a handkerchief. Did he have an accent?

If she recognized the voice, she could warn Zach. Then, even if—

She couldn't go there.

"The police are on the way," she shouted, trying to sound assertive and in control. "They'll apprehend you. You won't get away with this."

The doorknob stopped moving. Had she scared him off?

Please, Lord.

She pressed her ear against the door, trying to make out the sound. A faint swish, barely audible over the peal of the security alarm, as if—

Even before her mind processed the sound, she leaped into the bathtub and screamed as round after round of gunfire splintered the door. Fragments of wood flew through the air, stinging her back and peppering her hands, which she'd wrapped protectively around her neck.

Ella trembled with fear. In a matter of seconds, he would push through the shattered doorway and turn his weapon on her where she huddled like a terrified child, hiding in the protective steel tub.

A siren mixed with the shrill of the alarm. Was her mind playing tricks on her?

Footsteps. Running toward her or away?

"Ella." Another voice.

Her heart lurched. "Zach!"

He was there, reaching for her, pulling her up and into his arms. "Are you hurt?"

She shook her head, struggled to speak and then fell against his chest and gasped for air, realizing she hadn't breathed since the door exploded.

"He…he tried to…kill me."

With his arm protectively around her, Zach guided her into her living room. She disarmed the security alarm. Silence filled the house.

"Did you see him?" Zach asked.

She shook her head. "No, but I heard his voice. It was muffled, but with an accent."

"French? German?"

"I'm not sure. Maybe one of the islands."

"Hawaii?"

"The Caribbean." She rubbed her neck. "How did the police—"

"Tyler called them as I left his house. A patrol car must have been in the area. Plus your security alarm sent a signal to the dispatcher."

Zach pulled out his cell phone and called police dispatch. "I'm at the Children's Care Clinic. A shooter tried to kill Dr. Jacobsen. He's on the run. Notify all units. Set up roadblocks. Comb the woods. He can't get away."

Disconnecting, Zach stared again into Ella's face. "You're sure you're okay?"

She nodded.

"Why didn't you call Levi?"

Tears welled in her eyes. "Oh, Zach, I did, but he was already in the house."

"You think Levi was the assailant?"

"I don't know, but why didn't he answer the phone?"

Zach wouldn't let Ella out of his sight again. He couldn't risk losing her. He kept thinking *What if?* What if his car hadn't started? What if there had been an accident on the road that delayed him? What if he hadn't gotten to her in time?

As it was, he'd floored the accelerator and fishtailed out of Tyler's drive. If anything had been in the road— a buggy, or a herd of cows that had broken out of their pasture—he would have arrived too late.

He fought the lump that filled his throat, thinking the unthinkable, and shoved his way back to the present.

The first officers to arrive on-site searched the woods behind the house. Tyler had alerted post. The military police joined with local law enforcement in setting up roadblocks.

They were dealing with more than a punk kid looking for the next high. The guy hadn't been searching for drugs. He'd been searching for Ella. To kill her.

Police interrogated Levi. They'd found him groggy with sleep in his house. Sarah, frightened and shaking, had confirmed that he'd been next to her in bed all night, and because of the distance between the two houses, they hadn't heard Ella's security alarm.

The cell phone that should have alerted him to Ella's distress had been inadvertently turned off. At least that was the alibi Levi used. He didn't know technology and had adjusted the volume of the ring so as not to disturb his wife. In reality, he had turned the cell off.

So much for Zach's good intentions, which had almost cost Ella her life.

As distraught as the pregnant Amish wife had been earlier in the day, Zach wondered if she might have tampered with the phone in order to ensure her husband could sleep through the night. Zach wasn't sure that Sarah had been forthright about her relationship with her brother. The two siblings could be working together, which meant Daniel Fisher could be the assailant.

Zach raked his hand through his hair and approached

Sergeant Abrams, who had interrogated Levi. "What's your assessment?" he asked.

"Levi seems sincere and is openly contrite about the phone."

"What about Sarah?"

The cop sniffed. "She's harder to read. I can't decide if she's sincere or playing us for fools. I've got two of my guys heading to her father's house to question the old man and haul his son in for interrogation. I'm holding Daniel for at least twenty-four hours this time."

Zach rubbed his chin. "All this could have started with his desire to destroy the twins' medical records, if he thought Levi was identified as the father. A breaking and entering escalates, and he turns his hatred for Levi against the doc."

Abrams nodded. "I've heard of stranger things happening. The guy's not wired tight, we know that. Add an overzealousness to defend his sister and anything could happen."

The cop glanced into the living room, where Ella sat, head in her hands. "How's she doing?"

"She's ready to collapse, but if you ask her, she'll say she's fine."

"Any need to take her back to the ER?"

Zach shook his head. "Not that I can determine. Something to calm her nerves might be beneficial, but I doubt she'd take anything more than ibuprofen. She's strong as a mule."

A corner of the cop's mouth twitched. "My suggestion, don't let her hear you make that comparison. The ladies I know wouldn't cotton to being compared to a domestic work animal."

Zach had to smile. "You're a wise man, Sergeant."

Abrams patted Zach's shoulder. "I'm not blind. Something's going on with you two. I'm not pointing a finger, but getting personally involved in a case makes for mistakes, if you get my drift."

Zach didn't know if he was being chastised or counseled. "I'm law enforcement first."

The cop slapped his shoulder. "I know you are. I'm just telling you what I see that maybe you don't. Freemont PD can handle the investigation. We'll keep you in the loop, but let us take the lead. You hover over the doc and be a first line of protection, while we track this guy down and apprehend him."

"You might be reading more into this?"

The sergeant stared at him. His eyes were filled with understanding and not the condemnation Zach had thought he might find. "I fell in love with my wife when I was working a case. It wasn't as big as this one, but I can read the signs."

Zach blew out a stiff breath.

Love?

Abrams had it all wrong. Yes, Zach felt a bit of attraction, but nothing more.

Ella glanced up, and their gazes met.

A warmth flooded over him, a feeling that was a bit disconcerting and took him by surprise. Maybe there was some truth to what the cop had said, after all.

"I'm going to Atlanta." Ella held the invitation to the symposium in her hand and waved it at Zach. "You're worried about my safety, but I'll be safer in Atlanta than around here."

She glanced at the policemen who were still combing through her house, looking for clues. "A man almost killed me. He broke into my clinic last night and he came after me again tonight. There's something he wants, and I'm afraid it's that he wants me dead."

Zach stood staring at her as if he wanted to talk her out of making the trip to the city.

"I won't tell anyone where I'm going," she rationalized. "The clinic is closed until Monday. I'll keep my cell on, and I'll call you when I arrive."

"I'm going with you."

"What?" She hadn't expected him to acquiesce so easily, which only proved he was as worried about her safety as she was.

"So you agree that I'll be safer in Atlanta?"

"I hope so. It doesn't seem to be working out so well around here."

The calmness in his voice and his dark gaze made her even more afraid. She had to face the truth that someone wanted to do her harm.

"I'll be all right, Zach. You don't need to go with me." Although as the words came out, she knew their folly. She did need Zach. She needed his arms to support her and his strong shoulders to lean on when the darkness became too intense.

He had come to her rescue once again, in the nick of time. If he hadn't...

She shivered, thinking of what could have happened, what had almost happened.

"I'm going with you," he repeated. "That's non-negotiable. I'll call the hotel and get a room across from yours. Tell the director that someone will accompany you. You can't go into the city alone, even if it seems a safer place than Freemont."

She knew he was right. "The invitation includes a guest, but I don't want anyone to know why you're with me."

"Tell them I'm interested in learning more about the research. Helping the local Amish has been a priority for the commanding general at Fort Rickman. I'll brief General Cameron when I return, so you'll be telling the truth."

"Your boss will let you off work?"

"I'll get a pass. That won't be a problem. I'll let Sergeant Abrams know, but I'll ask him to keep the information to himself."

"You suspect someone in law enforcement?"

"Not at this point, but the fewer individuals who know your whereabouts, the better."

"What about Sarah Miller, in case she needs medical care?"

"She could be involved, Ella."

"That's ridiculous. Do you suspect Levi, as well?"

"I'm more prone to question his wife's motives because of her brother."

Ella turned away and hung her head. Zach's words cut into her heart. What had she done by coming to Freemont? She was destroying a young couple who had done nothing wrong.

Letting out a deep sigh, she turned back to Zach. "I'll call the director and let her know. We can leave tomorrow morning."

"You can't stay here tonight."

"Maybe I can stay with Wendy or my receptionist."

Tyler stepped into the room. He had evidently heard the last portion of their conversation. "You need a place to stay?" he asked.

"I do."

"My fiancée has room at her house." Tyler moved closer. "I'm sure Carrie won't mind. Zach and I can keep watch throughout the night."

"Sounds good," Zach said. "I'll head to my BOQ first thing in the morning and pack a bag for Atlanta. I also want to stop at CID headquarters and brief the chief before he heads to the airport."

Tyler pulled out his phone. "I'll call Carrie and confirm the plans with her. There shouldn't be a problem."

Once he had left the room, Zach took Ella's hand.

"This won't last forever," he said, as if he could sense her unease. "The local police will track down the attacker. Or he'll make a mistake, and they'll catch him before—"

She stared at Zach, knowing what he was thinking but couldn't say out loud.

There would be a next time. She wasn't safe anywhere, and if the police didn't put the pieces together fast enough, the next time could be fatal.

Then a thought caught at her heart. What if the danger that confronted her turned on Zach? What if something happened to him when he was trying to protect her?

The assailant had to be stopped. Before he hurt Ella, and even more important, before he harmed Zach.

FOURTEEN

"You've been too gracious," Ella said as she hugged Carrie goodbye the next morning, and then handed her bag to Zach.

"Anytime you need a place to stay," Tyler's fiancée said, "don't hesitate to call me."

Ella nodded and then hugged Tyler. "You and Zach did a good job keeping the ladies safe last night, but I don't think either of you slept."

He smiled and shrugged. "Zach and I are used to running on no sleep. Plus we spelled each other for an hour or two."

As Zach placed Ella's luggage in his car, Tyler added, "I needed to force him to grab a few *z*'s. I don't think Zach's slept in days. Keep talking as you drive to Atlanta to keep him awake."

She laughed. "I'll be a chatterbox. He'll ask me to shut up."

"I doubt that." Tyler looked at her knowingly, as if he realized something special had developed between them. Was it that obvious?

After saying their goodbyes, Ella slid into the passenger seat, nodding her thanks to Zach before he closed the door and hurried to the driver's side.

They both waved, and as they drove away, Ella turned

to watch Tyler and Carrie fade from view. "They're a great couple, and they had high praise for you, Zach."

He smiled and turned onto the road that would take them into Freemont and then to the interstate. "They're good people. I thought they'd be married by now, but they're both taking their time and getting to know each other, which is probably smart."

"Carrie said it wouldn't be long."

"Tyler insisted I get some shut-eye last night. You probably coerced him into taking care of me."

Ella held up her hands and laughed. "I plead innocent. He recognized the fatigue lining your eyes. He's a smart guy who wanted to help out. Friends like that are hard to find."

"You're right."

She patted his hand. "I'm relieved you got some rest. I must admit that I slept, as well. Probably for the first time since the attack."

She glanced out the window and then asked, "Have you learned anything new about Mary Kate's condition?"

"She's responding to treatment, so evidently there's improvement."

"Which is what we want. Did you contact Corporal Powers's unit?"

"They're keeping him under watch, although he's allowed to visit his wife at the hospital. The main concern is that he might do something rash and hurt himself. They don't seem to think that he'll hurt anyone else."

"That's a tough way to come home from a war zone."

"The counselors and medical personnel working with our PTSD soldiers are top of the line. I'm satisfied that he's getting the best care possible."

"What about Mary Kate?" Ella asked.

"The military hospital at Fort Freemont is staffed with

highly competent physicians and other medical personnel. Mary Kate will pull through."

Ella shook her head. "I don't want to think of what could happen.

"They're doing everything possible to ensure she improves."

"I'm sure they are." Ella glanced at Zach. "Before you, I had never known anyone who was career army."

"What's your assessment now that you know me?"

She hesitated, weighing her words. "You're a great guy, Zach, with a big heart. Even though you try to put up a tough front, down deep you're a softy."

"Is that right?" He laughed, causing her heart to flutter. "That's somewhat like the way I see you." He flicked a quick glance at her before he turned his eyes back to the road. "You're ever the medical expert, spouting information and speaking in long sentences."

"Really?" Her cheeks burned.

"Maybe you feel the need to prove yourself. But…" He hesitated a moment. "I don't see a medical professional when I look at you. I see a very interesting lady with a big heart who must love children and wants to make the world a better place. Your husband was the intellectual. You were the heart."

Moved by Zach's comment, Ella glanced out the window.

He touched her hand. "Am I right?"

She turned back to face him, seeing the openness of his gaze. "You said I was perceptive, Zach, but you seem to be, as well."

"An investigator puts the pieces together. You've mentioned your husband a number of times. All I did was make the connections."

"Just as you said, Quin was all head. I like to think that

I am more heart. Unfortunately, we couldn't seem to find a midpoint that worked for both of us."

"I'm sorry." Again, Zach reached for her hand, only this time he didn't let go.

The highway stretched before them, taking them to Atlanta for a symposium that would highlight her husband's work.

Zach was right; for all her attempts to appear strong, she was apprehensive about what the day would bring. She appreciated the warmth of his touch and was grateful for his friendship and support.

But wasn't it more than friendship? Something much more? The special agent with the understanding gaze had wormed his way into her heart.

Confronting the medical research team who had worked with Quin would be a challenge. Thankfully, Zach was with her. No matter how strong she tried to be, she couldn't have faced them alone.

Navigating Atlanta traffic made Zach realize he was a country boy at heart. Even early in the day, the connector that led into the heart of the city was sixteen lanes of bumper-to-bumper traffic.

At least the front desk personnel at the hotel were accommodating. He had requested a room across from Ella's when he'd made his reservation, but he'd ended up on the twelfth floor, while she was on the seventh. Thankfully, the staff was able to make the change, which placed Zach three rooms away from her.

"You're worried about my safety," she said as they rode up in the elevator.

"I can't turn off being a special agent," he answered, although there was far more to it than that. Someone was out to do Ella harm. Even though she had left Freemont, and hopefully, the danger remained there, Zach wouldn't let down his guard.

"Let's stick together, okay?" he said with a smile. "Then I won't have to worry quite so much."

"Did you want to check my room to make sure no one's hiding in there?" Her comment was offhand, but Zach realized she understood the importance of being cautious.

"Now you're thinking like someone in law enforcement." He took the key from her, swiped it against the sensory pad on the door and stepped into the room. Quickly, he checked the closet and bathroom and under the bed, before motioning her inside.

"Everything looks fine," he assured her. "I'll be three doors down on the opposite side of the hallway. Room 712. What time do we need to head to the symposium?"

"Let me check the welcome packet." The large manila envelope had been waiting at the front desk for Ella. She pulled out a number of papers and searched through them.

"I found the information," she said. "The symposium's being held in Decatur. Due to a lack of parking, they ask everyone to use MARTA, the city's mass transit system. The station's not far from here."

"What time should we leave?"

She glanced at another paper and pointed to a paragraph halfway down the printout. "Nancy's scheduled to speak about CED at 1:00 p.m., immediately after the lunch break. Why don't we leave here at eleven fifteen? We'll arrive at the symposium ahead of schedule and grab lunch there before the talk."

Zach checked his watch. "I'll knock on your door in an hour. Don't forget to engage both locks, and don't open the door to anyone. I'm going to scout out the hotel. You can reach me on my cell." He pointed to the printout with the schedule of events. "Mind if I take a look at where we'll be later today?"

She handed him the information. "You take it. The dinner and program will be held in the Magnolia Ballroom, here in this hotel."

"I'll find it." Stepping into the hallway, he waited outside her door until she had engaged the security bolt.

His own room was a mirror image of Ella's. He left his luggage inside and then followed the hallway to the stairwell and went down to the third floor, where the ballrooms were located.

Once he knew the layout for the evening event, and the various elevators and stairways, he returned to his room and called Sergeant Abrams.

"Anything new on Daniel Fisher?" Zach asked.

"Nothing from Alabama, but we've got something on him from Florida. Guess he headed to the Sarasota area last year. Daniel rented a room and left without paying his bill. I'm still digging, but at least that gives me a reason to hold him. I'm counting on him coming clean about the attack on the doc. He's got an angry edge and a sense of entitlement. The world owes him. Why, I'm not sure."

"Let me know if you do have to release him."

"How's Atlanta?" Abrams asked.

"Crowded with people and overflowing with traffic. They suggest we take MARTA to the medical talk, which is probably a good idea."

"I'm glad you're with the doc. She's probably safer in Atlanta than she would be at her clinic, but you never know. She needs someone watching her back."

"I'll call you when we return tomorrow."

"Stay safe, Zach."

"Right." He disconnected. The most important thing was to keep Ella safe.

Why was she on edge?

Ella hadn't expected the anxiety that welled up within

her as she and Zach left the hotel. She glanced at her watch. They had plenty of time to get to the symposium and grab a sandwich or salad before the presentation.

Zach took her arm and guided her along the sidewalk. "There's the MARTA station." He pointed to an entrance just ahead.

They hurried down the stairs to the platform, which was awash with a mix of people, from men and women in business suits, to college students and blue-collar workers, to street folks, all of whom relied on MARTA for transportation within the city.

Ella pointed to a train that was loading. "Is that the one we need to take?"

Zach shook his head. "We've got about ten minutes before the Decatur train arrives."

Ella weaved her way through the crowd and stopped not far from the edge of the platform. She peered over the drop-off and stared down, approximately four feet, to the tracks below.

"Better not get too close," Zach warned, wrapping his hand protectively around her elbow.

"Just trying to see how the cars are powered. I went to school in Columbus, Ohio, but I still consider myself a country girl. I've never been around mass transit systems."

Zach pointed to an outside rail covered partially with a metal sheath. "That's the conductor rail, also known as the third rail. The trains have what's called a 'shoe' that slides over it and transfers power to the engine's electric motor."

"Remind me not to walk on any MARTA tracks."

"Folks have died who haven't realized the danger, or who..." He looked at her as if he'd said the wrong thing.

...*who wanted to end their lives*. Mentally, she completed his thought.

Quin hadn't taken his own life, no matter what the

Memphis cops had told Zach. Frustrated, Ella pulled out of his hold and wrapped her arms around her waist.

Zach pointed to a train schedule posted on the wall. "We want the blue line heading east."

His phone trilled. He checked the caller ID on his cell and shrugged. "No name, just a number."

He raised the phone to his ear. "Special Agent Zach Swain." His brow furrowed, and he turned his head to the side. "Could you repeat that?" He glanced at Ella and pointed to a corner alcove away from the crowd.

She nodded, knowing he'd be able to hear more clearly away from the people who packed the platform.

Ella again glanced down at the tracks. A group of kids holding skateboards shoved past her.

"Watch out," she warned, for their safety as well as hers.

A swell of new arrivals hurried down the steps and filled the platform, forcing her dangerously close to the edge. Someone pushed against her. She struggled to keep her balance.

"Stop," she cried, feeling propelled forward. Her heart lurched. Her arms flailed as another shove sent her over the lip.

She screamed and fell to the tracks below, her shoulder and hip taking the brunt of the fall. Gasping, she struggled to sit up, her hand coming close to the live rail.

"Someone's on the track!" a bystander shrieked.

Ella looked up, dazed, realizing people were pointing at her.

A roar filled her ears. The ground rumbled.

She peered down the track and saw nothing, then, glancing over her shoulder, discovered a huge train barreling down upon her.

Her heart pounded at breakneck speed. She tried to move, but her body failed to respond. Knowing she'd be crushed by the giant rail car, she opened her mouth to scream again. The sound caught in her throat. She couldn't breathe, and all she could hear was the roar of the train.

"Ella!"

Zach jumped from the platform. He grabbed her shoulders and rolled her away from the rail and into a narrow recessed area under the platform. Nestled in his arms, she heard the terrible rumble, louder than a bomb exploding around them. She closed her eyes and buried her face in his chest, too afraid to cry, too panicked to think or move or do anything but cling to Zach, who had pulled her from danger.

Just that quickly, the train passed.

"Are you hurt?" he asked, his voice husky with emotion. He pulled back ever so slightly to look into her eyes.

She shook her head, unable to speak and unwilling to leave the security of his arms.

"Hurry." He helped her out of the protective area. "We have to get to safety before the next train arrives."

People on the platform stood back, as if unable to believe they had survived.

"I need some help," Zach demanded.

Hands reached down and pulled her to safety. Zach climbed up behind her. Trembling, Ella clung to him, unwilling to let go of the man who had saved her once again.

"What happened?" he asked.

She shook her head, unable to come to terms with what had just occurred. "Someone…someone shoved against me," she finally said.

Her eyes scanned the crowd. Was the person still on the platform?

"Were you pushed?" Zach asked.

"I—I'm not sure. Pushed, or maybe it was the number of people. With the crowd moving forward, I was caught in the swell…"

He turned to study the crowd, just as she had done.

"It was an accident," a man standing near them told his friend.

But Ella had felt the pressure on her back. Someone had wanted her to fall. Someone had known the train was approaching, and he'd shoved her off the platform.

FIFTEEN

Zach should have known the Atlanta police wouldn't be convinced that someone had tried to kill Ella. At least the officer took down the information and seemed relieved that she had survived.

"You're fortunate, ma'am," he said, as if Ella didn't realize death had been a breath away.

He turned to Zach. "Sir, you did the right thing. That space under the platform is an emergency area in case someone falls onto the tracks. Glad it offered the protection you needed. You know about the third rail?"

Zach nodded, thinking of how close Ella had been to the live power source. His heart pounded as he recalled hearing the shouts of the onlookers and realizing, almost too late, what had happened.

Seeing the approaching train, and Ella lying paralyzed on the track, he didn't have time to think; all he could do was react.

As the memory flashed through his mind again, Zach put his arm around her and let out a stiff breath.

The cop stared at him for a moment. "You okay, sir?"

"It was a close call."

"Yes, sir. You got that right." He turned to Ella. "Regrettably, the security camera in this area of the platform is broken. Unless you can identify the person who shoved you, ma'am, there's nothing the Atlanta PD can do at this point. I encourage you to be vigilant and on guard."

He handed both of them his card. "Don't hesitate to contact me if you think of anything else that might have a bearing on what happened, or if you feel threatened in any way."

"Thanks, Officer."

"Where are you folks headed?"

Ella told him the location of the symposium.

"I'm going that way. I'd be happy to drive you there. After what you just experienced, I have a feeling the last place you want to be is on a MARTA train."

Zach appreciated the officer's thoughtfulness and thanked him profusely when he dropped them at their destination.

"Let me know anytime you're in south Georgia," Zach said as he shook the man's hand. "I'll show you around Fort Rickman. We've got a nice museum, lovely Amish community and a friendly town, called Freemont. The fishing's good in the river that runs through the area, as well as a lake that's not far from post." He gave the officer his card.

"I'll take you up on the fishing," the cop said with a smile. "You folks stay safe."

As he drove away, Zach glanced at his watch. "It's twelve forty-five," he told Ella. "I doubt we have time to grab some lunch."

"Not if we want to hear Nancy speak. We can wait until afterward to eat, but I'd like to clean up a bit in the ladies' room."

She patted her purse. "And I'm still grateful for the Good Samaritan who retrieved and returned my handbag."

They hurried into the building. Ten minutes later, Zach ushered a freshly cleaned-up Ella into the presentation room and toward two seats on the far aisle, where he would have a clear view of both the crowd and the door.

The director was tall and slender and wore a wide smile as she hurried to give Ella what appeared to be a sincere hug of greeting.

"It's wonderful to see you," the woman said, her gaze warm and welcoming. "I know you probably think I twisted your arm, but I wanted to have Quin represented with the rest of the team. He did so much on this project."

"Thank you." Ella introduced Zach.

"Nice to meet you, ma'am."

"You're a friend of Ella's?" Nancy Vaughn's eyebrows rose ever so slightly.

"We met recently, and Dr. Jacobsen thought I might be interested in learning more about your Amish Project. I'll be sharing the information with the commanding general when I return to Fort Rickman. He's committed to improving relations between the military and civilian communities, especially our Amish neighbors. If there's anything we can do to help you folks while you're in Georgia, please don't hesitate to ask."

"Thank you so much, Special Agent Swain. I'm having a gathering in my hotel suite before dinner this evening," the director said. "It's listed on the program Ella received. I hope you'll join us."

He smiled. "If Dr. Jacobsen is there, I will be, as well."

"Wonderful. Now I'd better get to the podium. Why don't you move closer to the front?"

Zach smiled again. "You're so thoughtful, but we'll be more than comfortable right here."

Nancy waved to a man who had just entered the room. "Ella, be sure to say hello to Ross. He, probably more than anyone, has felt the loss of Quin's passing, as you can imagine."

Tilting her head toward Zach, the director added, "Quin

and Dr. Underwood worked together. They were a good team. Losing Quin was like losing a friend and a brother, as well as a fellow researcher."

The man approached. He was six-two, well built and handsome, and for half a second Zach was jealous when he put his arms around Ella and kissed her cheek.

"It's been too long," the researcher said.

"Pennsylvania is far from Georgia, Ross. I'm glad you decided to release your findings closer to my new home."

"With the Centers for Disease Control and Prevention in Atlanta, we knew many of their scientists would be interested. The medical symposium was already scheduled, so we piggybacked on their event. Of course, they were most gracious about fitting us in, knowing the importance of the Amish Project. I just wish…"

He paused and smiled. "Well, you know how I felt about Quin. If only he could be here with us today."

"That's kind of you to say." Ella seemed a bit flustered. Perhaps the mention of her husband brought back too many memories.

She introduced Zach.

"Nice meeting you, Mr. Swain." After kissing Ella's cheek again, Underwood joined the director near the podium.

Ella smiled at a number of people who streamed into the room. "You made points with Nancy," she said to Zach. "But are you sure the commanding general would be interested in the Amish Project?"

"He's a very philanthropic guy. His wife started a craft fair with the Amish, and they both love kids, so you never know. Plus I didn't want the director to ask any more questions. I'd prefer her to think I'm here as a friend and not as a CID agent."

"Thank you again, Zach, for protecting me. I'm losing count of the number of times you've saved my life."

Ella smiled at him, then turned her attention to the front as the director was introduced.

Zach followed the introductions and explanation of the preliminary work that had been done on the project. But when the director mentioned various enzyme deficiencies and how they played into the molecular and physiological well-being of the children, he turned his attention to their surroundings rather than the medical discussion.

He glanced at everyone who entered the room, and searched the audience for someone, anyone, who looked suspect. Ella was in danger, even in Atlanta, and he had to be on guard to keep her safe.

When Nancy Vaughn finished speaking, she was soon surrounded by many members of the audience, individuals who probably wanted to offer congratulations or ask follow-up questions.

"Let's go," Ella said to Zach.

"Did you want to talk to anyone else?" he asked, glancing around at the crowd.

She followed his gaze. Some of the people hurriedly left the room, perhaps moving on to the next presentation on the agenda. Others mulled about, chatting among themselves.

Ian Webb stood near the door. He smiled and headed her way. She extended her hand as he neared. "Ian, it's good to see you."

"Ella, a pleasure as always. The director mentioned that she had dropped an invitation to you in the post. I had hoped to see you, but you left Carlisle before I had a chance to stop by."

"I needed to move on with my life. I hope you understand."

"Be assured that I do." He glanced at Zach.

Ella made the introductions and again provided a reason for Zach accompanying her. "The military is interested in helping the Amish community where my clinic is located. I thought the symposium, and this talk especially, would shed light on the work being done with genetic diseases that impact Amish children."

Ian nodded. "Our hope from the onset has been to increase public awareness." He glanced at his watch. "I'm off to another lecture. I'll see you tonight?"

"We plan to attend."

"Till then." The Brit made his way from the room.

Ella watched him leave. "Ian was my husband's assistant," she told Zach. "I think he's a great guy, although Quin sometimes saw him in a different light." She smiled sheepishly. "As you've probably picked up from the comments I've made, my husband was faint on praise."

"Where's Webb from? I noticed his accent."

"Somewhere in the UK."

"The assailant last night had a muffled voice, and you mentioned an accent. Could it have been British?"

Ella shook her head. Zach had jumped to the wrong conclusion. "Ian is a good man," she insisted. "It wasn't his voice I heard."

"Are you sure?"

A chill settled over her. She couldn't be certain of Ian. Couldn't be certain of anyone right now.

Maybe coming to Atlanta had been a mistake, if danger had followed her here. She glanced at Zach, who had left her on the train platform to answer a phone call. Could he have returned unnoticed in the midst of the crowd? Could her protector also be her assailant?

She shook her head, unwilling to think such thoughts. What was wrong with her? She was seeing danger everywhere, even in a man who had warmed a place in her heart.

Not Zach. He was her protector, and he'd saved her life

more than once. She owed him her gratitude and appreciation. But what about Ian? What motive would he have?

She thought of Quin's files. Was there something hidden that needed to be revealed? After she got home tomorrow, she'd unpack his office records and work her way through each scrap of information, looking for some clue as to why she was under attack. Until then, she needed to keep up her guard.

Zach took her arm and escorted her out of the room. Did she need to be on guard even around him?

"You need to eat," Zach insisted, as they left the symposium.

"I'm not hungry."

"Maybe not, but your body needs fuel, Ella. I would think a doctor would understand the importance of good nutrition. What would you tell a patient who refused to eat?"

"I'd tell them they wouldn't get well without nourishment, but I'm not sick."

"You're running on empty, and you've been through a lot. Stress can wear a person down as much as illness."

She sighed. "You're right, of course."

Stepping outside, Zach spied a sandwich shop on the next block. "Let's head across the street. It won't take long. Then we can catch a cab back to the hotel."

"You don't want to chance MARTA?"

"Do you?"

She shook her head. "A MARTA station is the last place I want to go."

"Then we'll take a taxi."

They both ordered a pastrami on rye and sweet tea.

"I never thought a Yankee would like sweet tea," Zach said with a laugh as she sipped from the chilled glass.

"And I wouldn't think a guy who lives in the South

would order pastrami." Ella took another drink of tea and then asked, "So where's home for you?"

"Wherever Uncle Sam sends me. But I grew up in Mobile, so you're right about me being a Southern boy."

"Without an accent."

"I've moved around a lot in the military. Along the way, I dropped the drawl."

They lingered over lunch, as if neither of them wanted to go back to the hotel. Tonight would be difficult for Ella, Zach felt sure. He'd noticed her tension during the medical address this afternoon. Something was bothering her, although she had yet to share what it could be.

Ella glanced at her watch. "It's almost three o'clock. We need to head to the hotel. The director invited us to a gathering of the research team in her suite, starting at 5:00 p.m. I'm not overly enthused about going, but I appreciate Nancy's thoughtfulness, and I need to attend." She looked at Zach. "You'll go with me?"

"Of course." He smiled and grabbed her hand, which was resting on the table. He'd intended the gesture to be a source of comfort, assuring her of his support and willingness to stand by her no matter where she needed to go.

But something happened as their palms touched. He felt it as surely as he felt the chair he was sitting on. A spark, an electric current, a jolt of power passed between them.

From the way Ella raised her gaze and inhaled sharply, it seemed she noticed it, as well. They sat, fingers entwined, as if time had stopped to give them this brief moment of connection.

Then their waitress interrupted them with the check. Ella hastily withdrew her hand while Zach paid the bill. He asked the server for the number of a local taxi service and made the call as soon as she provided it.

"Thanks for a delicious lunch," Ella said as they walked outside.

The serenity of their leisurely meal quickly evaporated as cars whizzed past them on the busy street. Zach moved protectively in front of Ella and kept his eyes peeled for anything that might look suspicious. A late model sports car carrying three older teens with long hair, tattoos and body piercings drove past. The bass on the vehicle's sound system thumped in the afternoon air.

Zach watched them pass and turn the corner. When they circled by again, he told Ella to step inside the restaurant, while he walked to the curb and stared at the driver.

The kid behind the wheel glared back before stomping on the accelerator and laying a black streak of rubber on the asphalt. Zach watched the car disappear from sight.

Relieved to see the punks drive off, he searched the block and focused on a man leaning against a storefront on the opposite side of the street. He had a folded newspaper under his arm, but made no attempt to read it. Instead, he pursed his lips and eyed Zach until the cab pulled to the curb.

Ella hurried from the sandwich shop and crawled into the rear seat. Before Zach slipped in next to her, he glanced again at the man across the street, who continued to stare at them.

"Do you know that guy?" Ella asked as Zach entered the cab.

"I've never seen him before. How about you?"

"No clue who he is or why he was watching us."

Watching you, Zach wanted to say, but he didn't need to alarm Ella any more.

The guy was midfifties, five-eleven, give or take an inch, probably 180 pounds, dressed in a flannel shirt and jeans. No reason to consider him a threat to Ella, except after what had happened, Zach didn't trust anyone. Not when her life was at stake. Everyone was suspicious, and everyone was a potential killer out to do her harm.

SIXTEEN

Ella hadn't expect Zach to look so handsome in his dress blue uniform. At some point, he had told her that CID special agents wore civilian clothes when working an investigation so that rank wouldn't interfere with any interrogations or questioning. She had thought the uniform rule would apply to their time in Atlanta, as well.

Instead he stood at her hotel room door looking bigger than life and twice as handsome as she remembered, even though they'd parted less than two hours ago.

"Blue becomes you," she said, struggling to find something to say that wouldn't give away the explosive emotions playing havoc with her heart.

"I hope you don't mind me wearing my uniform."

"I think it's the perfect attire."

He smiled and then dropped his gaze, as if taking in the little black cocktail dress she wore.

"I should have brought a bouquet of flowers to present to the beautiful woman who graced me with her presence tonight. As we often say around the office, you've made my day."

She laughed. "Is that a compliment?"

"Why, yes, ma'am, that's definitely a compliment, but if you have any doubts, let me rephrase my statement."

His eyes twinkled, making him look even more alluring.

"Dr. Jacobsen, you look stunning, and I'm humbled and honored to be escorting you this evening. If you're ready, ma'am?" He extended his arm.

She locked hers with his and laughed, feeling a burst of excitement that displaced her apprehension. Earlier she had fretted about what the night would bring, but Zach made her feel special and attractive. Something she hadn't felt for a very long time.

They walked arm in arm to the elevator and rode to the penthouse. "I'm more relaxed," she admitted. "The danger has passed, at least for tonight."

Zach nodded, although his eyes told a different story. He was still on guard and worried about her safety. He squeezed her hand as the elevator doors opened and they headed to the director's suite.

"Stay close." He tapped on the door. "If you feel threatened in any way, just tell me you're tired. That will be our code, and we'll leave immediately." He stared into her eyes. "Understand?"

She nodded as the door opened. The director glanced at Ella and then Zach, and hesitated for an instant before she invited them in. "Welcome. I'm so glad you both could join us this evening."

They followed her into the living room of the massive suite, where a number of people were gathered around a large table covered with trays of hors d'oeuvres.

"Tell the bartender what you and Ella would like to drink," Nancy said to Zach.

"Club soda with a twist of lime for me," Ella said.

"Make that two," he told the bartender.

Ross Underwood approached. "So glad you and Zach could be with us."

"I'm grateful Nancy included us." Ella accepted the drink Zach handed her. "You know Special Agent Swain."

Ross stuck out his hand. "The director said the general at Fort Rickman is interested in the health of the Amish children near your military post."

"General Cameron is interested in fostering good relations with all our civilian neighbors."

"Which I didn't expect from the military." The researcher turned abruptly back to Ella. "I hope you found the director's announcements today to be encouraging. She said you'd had twin patients with the same symptoms."

Ella nodded. "I called some months ago, when the children first came in for an evaluation. I wanted to ensure that Quin's treatment protocol, the one he established, was still the treatment of choice. Nancy said it was."

"How are the girls faring?"

"The results have been quite startling and so encouraging. With proper management, they should have a normal childhood and productive lives. Nancy said you're leading the team. Congratulations." The position Quin had held, although Ella didn't need to state what they both knew.

"Nancy encouraged me to take over after Quin's untimely death," Ross explained. "You know how upset I was. His were big shoes to fill, and of course, the work is never the result of any one person, but rather the efforts of the entire group."

A *tap-tap-tap* sounded at the door, and Ian Webb entered. He waved to the director, patted Ross on the back and then extended his hand to Ella and Zach. "Good to see you both again."

"We were just discussing Quin's contribution to the team." Ross brought the newcomer into the conversation.

"Your husband was a dedicated researcher," Ian told Ella. "He loved his work, although something has troubled me." She stepped closer to both men and lowered her voice. "Quin had been upset shortly before his death because of some results he'd received. He said three sets of twins were involved."

Ross frowned thoughtfully. "We only had one set of twins as I recall, the Zook children." He looked with questioning eyes at Ella. "Are you referring to this study or to something earlier?"

"The last study Quin worked on. Surely you remember the twins. Quin kept pictures of the children in his office."

She turned to Ian. "Do you remember them?"

"I'd have to check my notes."

"Ross?" Nancy motioned to him from across the table. "Excuse me for a minute."

Ian reached for a cracker from a tray, scooped up a large dollop of dip and popped it into his mouth. Soon afterward, his eyes widened and he reached for a second cracker.

"The dip's fantastic," he said. "A cream cheese base, garlic, onion, a dash or two of Tabasco and something else that I can't identify."

"It looks good." Zach grabbed a cracker. "I'll give it a try."

"The chef calls it a seafood spread," the bartender said as he handed Ian the glass of wine he had requested.

Ian turned to Ella. "Aren't you allergic to some type of seafood? Was it shrimp?"

She nodded. "Crab, but I stay away from shellfish of any kind."

"Then don't follow my lead," he insisted. "Nancy left the menu details to her secretary, who probably didn't know about your allergy."

Zach dropped the cracker he'd loaded with dip onto a cocktail napkin and reached for a piece of cheddar cheese instead.

Ella noticed the switch. "You don't like seafood?" she asked.

"My mother was allergic to shrimp. The doctor told me I could inherit her sensitivity. I've never been tested, so I just stay away from anything that comes from the sea."

Ian's brow furrowed. "You don't know whether you're allergic?"

Zach shrugged. "You don't miss what you've never had."

"Exactly right, my good man. Plus if you don't eat the dip, it leaves more for me." Ian laughed heartily as he fixed another cracker.

Nancy tapped her wineglass with a spoon, getting everyone's attention. "I just want to say a few words of thanks to this wonderful team that has worked successfully and achieved an amazing breakthrough in medical science."

She glanced about the room at the twenty or so scientists and guests who crowded around the table. "Your hard work and persistence even when the results weren't always positive, especially early on, made the difference." She glanced at Ella. "We lost a strong member of the team, and his death may have encouraged all of us to work harder."

Ella's cheeks burned.

"Each life is important, and the children who are being helped would not have survived without Quin's hard work and the treatment protocol he established."

The director glanced at the people gathered in the room. Pride was evident in her gaze. "Join me in a toast to the Amish Project. May this lead us to new breakthroughs, so even more children can enjoy healthy, productive lives." She raised her glass. "To the research center and the successful completion of this project. May we never stop working for the betterment of mankind and the health of children, especially Amish children."

Everyone raised their glasses. Shouts of "Hear, hear!" echoed around the room.

Ross held his glass up again. "Join me in a toast to Quin Jacobsen and his significant contribution to the Amish Project."

Touched by Ross's thoughtfulness, Ella raised her glass. Zach stood next to her and followed suit. "To Quin Jacobsen."

"And now," the director said, "we need to proceed to the main ballroom to welcome our guests. As you know, the monies raised at this dinner will help cover the cost of care for many of our patients who lack insurance. The revenue will pay for their treatment and medication. Join me in welcoming the guests and thanking them for their contributions to our Healing Fund."

As the scientists finished their drinks and headed for the door, Ross approached Ella. "I am glad you're here today. I'm sure Quin would be honored, as well."

"Thank you for the toast, Ross. That was gracious and kind."

"I always admired Quin. He had a great mind and a gift for getting to the heart of a problem and finding a solution in a timely manner."

"Your words bring me comfort." Ella smiled with appreciation. "I'm grateful."

She and Zach took the elevator down to the third floor. They found their names on the seating chart posted outside the ballroom. They had been placed at one of the head tables, with some of the researchers. Ella was glad to see that Ian Webb would be with them.

Looking around the ballroom, she took in the ornate chandeliers and lovely flower arrangements. Many ladies wore flowing dresses, some decorated with sequins that glittered in the candlelight from the tables.

"Everyone looks so beautiful," she told Zach as guests

streamed into the ballroom. The men were handsomely dressed, but no one looked as dashing as he did.

"You're the most beautiful woman here, Ella."

Surprised by Zach's comment, she felt her cheeks flush, although deep down, she was pleased by the compliment. Swept up in the moment as she was, the MARTA incident and break-in at her clinic seemed long ago.

"May I get you something to drink?" he asked.

"I'm fine. Just enjoying the grandeur."

"And I'm enjoying you. Should we considered this a date, even though *you* asked *me*?" His lips twitched with mischief.

She widened her eyes. "You *told* me you were accompanying me to Atlanta."

"Should I have stayed in Freemont?"

"No." She shook her head. "I'm very glad you're here."

Catching sight of a familiar face, she poked Zach's arm and pointed to the door. "Look who just entered the ballroom."

Zach's eyes flicked over the guests until he saw someone who made him pause. "The twins' grandfather, Mr. Landers."

"What's he doing here?" she asked.

"I'm ready to find out. Wait here, Ella."

She shook her head. "No, I'm going with you, Zach."

The older gentlemen looked surprised when they approached him. "I didn't expect to see either of you tonight," he said as a curt greeting.

"Sir." Ella extended her hand. Mr. Landers shook it and then Zach's.

"My husband was involved in the research team that first identified CED, the disease your granddaughters have," Ella explained. "I was invited because of my husband, and I asked Special Agent Swain to join me. How did you learn about the event?"

"Through the organization that raises money for children who can't pay for their treatments. My wife made reservations some weeks ago to attend tonight's dinner. Of course, with our daughter in the hospital, Lucy needed to stay with the girls. I'm here to make a contribution and to thank the research team."

He lowered his gaze. "Seems I need to thank you, Dr. Jacobsen, for diagnosing the girls' condition and for making me realize that I was wrong about Levi Miller."

"In what way, Mr. Landers?"

"I've always had hard feelings toward the Amish because they didn't accept me when I wanted to marry Lucy. It broke her heart to leave her family, but she did it because she loved me. Eventually, we moved to Freemont to be close to Amish folks, although I never made an effort to get to know any of them. And I was especially hateful toward Levi. I forbade Mary Kate from seeing him when she was a teen. I might have saved all of us a lot of heartache if I hadn't been so bullheaded."

His eyes were filled with contrition when he looked up. "It was easier to see the fault in Levi, rather than accepting that I was wrong. It broke my heart to see Mary Kate make the same mistakes that her mother and I did. The Lord blessed us with the twins, but now my daughter's in the hospital and my son-in-law's got more on his shoulders than anyone should have to carry."

"How is Mary Kate?" Ella asked.

"There's a little improvement, but I'm still worried she won't survive."

Ella's heart went out to the troubled father. "Holding on to hope is important, Mr. Landers."

"Hugh's with her now. He'll head to the house later. The nurses said they'll call him if she takes a turn for the worse."

"How's his outlook?"

"Not good." Mr. Landers sighed. "He got into an argument with one of the doctors. A couple of the medics had to hold Hugh back so it didn't turn into something physical. The doc said he needs medical help, which only made matters worse. Hugh's discouraged and worried out of his mind."

That's what Ella feared.

"Do you think it's wise to have him with the girls, especially with his escalating outbursts? He's their father, but a lot has happened." She glanced at Zach, who picked up on her concern.

"He wasn't supposed to leave post," Zach said. "I'll call his unit. He needs to stay in the barracks tonight. He'll be closer to the hospital and able to get to Mary Kate more quickly if there is a problem."

"That sounds like a good solution." Ella remained with Mr. Landers as Zach stepped into the hallway and made the call.

He returned and nodded. "The first sergeant will see to it. He's heading to the hospital now and will drive Corporal Powers back to the barracks."

"But will he go willingly?" Ella wondered.

She glanced from Zach to Mr. Landers, but neither man looked optimistic.

"I'll thank everyone now and head home immediately after dinner," Mr. Landers said. "You've got me worried about my wife and the girls. I've always had a good relationship with my son-in-law, but he came back a different man."

"Sir, why don't you call your wife," Zach suggested. "Tell her to keep her doors locked and the phone number for the Freemont police department close at hand. It might be overkill, but I'd rather be safe than sorry."

"You're right, Zach. That's good advice." The strain

on Mr. Landers's face revealed how worried he was about his family.

Keep the girls safe.

The words flashed through Ella's mind. A thought? Or a prayer? If it was a prayer, would the Lord listen? And if He heard her, would He also respond?

SEVENTEEN

Ella escorted Mr. Landers to the head table and introduced him to the director. While they talked, Zach went into the hallway and called Sergeant Abrams.

After explaining his concern about Corporal Powers, Zach added, "If you can, have one of your cars patrol around the Landerses' home. The first sergeant plans to keep Powers overnight in the barracks, but things can change. I wanted you to be aware of the situation."

"Thanks for the information. We'll watch the house. I wouldn't want anything to happen to those little girls or to their grandmother. Hate to think that their father would do something to harm them, but we've seen the results of PTSD before this. What time do you plan to return to Freemont tomorrow?"

"By early afternoon. I'll call you when we arrive."

"And I'll let you know if anything changes around here."

Zach disconnected and found Ella standing near their table. She shared that Mr. Landers had given the director a sizable check to help their research continue. "He embarrassed me by saying that I had saved his granddaughters. I told him I wasn't the one to thank."

"You're too humble, Ella."

"The thanks goes to my husband and the members of

the research team who made the breakthrough, which I mentioned to Mr. Landers."

She seemed more positive about her husband, Zach noted. Being back in the environment of researchers and physicians—her peers—probably gave her a renewed appreciation for what he had accomplished.

"Your husband must have been a brilliant physician," Zach said, feeling a tug of sadness. It hadn't been that long ago when Ella had allowed Zach to take her hand, had relied on him to keep her safe.

The director moved to the podium. "Ladies and gentlemen, if you would take your seats at this time, please."

Zach helped Ella with her chair and shook hands with the other people sitting at the table. They worked at the center, but in other areas of research, all except Ian.

Ella had mentioned the assailant's accent. While it seemed unlikely that the British researcher could be involved in the clinic break-in, Zach had learned long ago to keep an open mind.

Ian sat on the other side of Ella. Too close for Zach's comfort, but he could do little to change the seating arrangement.

The director tapped the microphone and the room quieted. "Ladies and gentlemen, I've asked Reverend Henry to lead us in an invocation."

The minister was tall and middle-aged, with a high forehead and long nose. "Father, we thank You for this gathering and for all that has been done in medical research to help children everywhere."

Zach glanced at Ella before he bowed his head. She seemed lost in prayer, and Zach wondered if he was wrong for not turning to the Lord.

God, I'm sorry. Forgive me for not making time for You in my life. Help me tonight to keep Ella safe.

Dinner was served following the invocation. Ella talked

to Ian and occasionally tried to bring Zach into the conversation. She ate the salad and roll, but ignored the main entrée when it was served.

"You're not hungry?" Zach asked.

"We had a late lunch," she offered as an explanation.

Perhaps she wasn't hungry because she was enjoying the British man at her side. Ian seemed to be the life of the party and his accent became more pronounced with each glass of wine.

After the dessert was served, the director stepped to the podium again. "We have a special treat tonight. I know you're here to celebrate all the work done at the clinic. Because of your generosity, young boys and girls will have access to the medical care they need." The audience applauded.

"I'd like to pay a tribute to those involved in our latest project. Please, sit back and enjoy the program."

The lights dimmed and a photo of Amish children at play appeared on the large television monitors positioned around the room. A series of photos showed the research team. Some were bent over microscopes, others were at their computers and still others were in the Amish community talking to families. The photographer, no doubt understanding the Amish aversion to snapshots, had remained at a distance. The faces of the children were hard to make out, but their distinctive clothing and the farmhouses in front of which they stood pointed to their simple lifestyle.

Ella stared at the video and sighed at the photos of the children. She pointed to a man carrying a young child in his arms. "That's Quin."

Ian patted her hand. "I'm sure it's hard to watch."

Her eyes brimmed with tears. Zach flicked his gaze from her to the British researcher, who seemed overly zealous. More pictures of Quin flashed on the monitor.

The final photo showed him surrounded by children, looking happy and upbeat and not the negative person Ella had described.

The years of his birth and death were superimposed over his photograph, followed by, "With gratitude for the contributions Dr. Quin Jacobsen made to the Amish Project."

The applause was instantaneous.

Nancy Vaughn moved to the microphone. "At this time, I'd like Dr. Ella Jacobsen, Quin's wife, to join me onstage."

Ella gasped. She patted her cheeks and fought back more tears. Zach stood and helped her with her chair.

Ian stood in turn and hugged her. "Well deserved, Ella. We're so glad you're here this evening to receive the award."

"Award? I…I never expected anything like this."

Zach squeezed her arm, but she hurried away from him and made her way to the stage.

Ross gave her his hand and steadied her as she climbed the steps to join the director at the podium. Nancy greeted her with open arms, and the two women embraced for a long moment as the applause continued.

Ella brushed her hand over her cheeks, wiping away tears, and accepted the etched crystal plaque engraved with the caduceus logo of the research center.

The director kept her arm around Ella and spoke into the microphone. "It is my honor and privilege to present this award for the inspiration, dedication and hard work of Dr. Quinton Jacobsen, who led the research team in the early days and contributed a great extent to the breakthrough in childhood enzyme deficiency. Ella, I am so grateful that you could join us this evening so we could recognize your husband posthumously for his involvement with the Amish Project."

Ella gripped the award to her heart and leaned toward

the microphone. "Thank you for this special honor for my husband." She glanced up. "I know Quin is looking down upon all of us and is appreciative of this expression of gratitude for his service. His work was his life. Thank you for recognizing him tonight."

Another round of applause accompanied Ella back to the table. Zach rose to help her with her chair, but she shook her head ever so slightly, grabbed her purse and hurried from the ballroom, still holding the award.

He excused himself from the table and hastened to catch up with her. She was standing in the hallway waiting for the elevator when he did so. Tears streamed from her eyes, and her grief seemed overwhelming.

Ella was mourning for a husband she still loved. Zach had been a fool to think that something could have developed between them. Her husband had died just eight months ago, hardly time for her to get over his passing.

The door to the elevator opened and they stepped in. Zach pushed the button for the seventh floor, handed her his handkerchief and then stood aside, hands folded in front of him, giving her space and a bit of privacy so she could continue grieving without him hovering too close.

The elevator stopped on their floor, and he walked her to her room, took the key from her hand and opened her door.

"We'll leave in the morning, Ella. What time shall I have the valet bring the car around to the front of the hotel?"

She shook her head. "I can't stay here. I need to go home."

"It's late," Zach reasoned. "You're tired." *And not thinking rationally*, he wanted to add, but seeing her troubled expression, he didn't voice his additional concern.

"I want to go home. There are boxes I need to unpack that belonged to Quin. There's a picture I want to find."

A picture of both of them, no doubt. As unsettled as she seemed, Zach knew going home was important to her.

"Give me fifteen minutes to change out of my uniform. Is that enough time for you?"

She nodded. "Knock on the door. I'll be packed and ready to go."

He hurried to his room, feeling heavyhearted. He'd made a mistake by getting emotionally involved with the doctor. He'd drive her home and ensure she was safe. Maybe he'd stand guard outside her clinic throughout the night.

Sergeant Abrams might have answers by now. Daniel Fisher could have confessed. Or perhaps Corporal Powers was somehow involved.

The end of the investigation was in sight; Zach could feel it as surely as he knew it was time to reel in his feelings and control his heart.

Once Tyler returned from his trip, Zach would ask him to take over the case. Zach needed to return to post. He didn't need to cause Ella any more problems.

Before he entered his hotel room, he turned and looked down the hallway, thinking of when he and Ella had first arrived and the sense of connection he'd felt when he was with her. How had he been so wrong?

Letting out a stiff breath, he entered the room and closed the door behind him. If only closing the door to his heart would be as easy.

Getting over Ella would take time, but he would succeed. He had to. He had no other choice than to say goodbye to her and to what he had hoped would develop between them.

What Zach had hoped for would never be.

Not now.

Not ever.

EIGHTEEN

Ella's heart was heavy as they drove back to Freemont. She stared into the dark night, her head turned away from Zach. She couldn't talk. Not tonight. Not after everything she had experienced in Atlanta.

The tribute to Quin had been unexpected. She'd set the crystal award at her feet in the car, unwilling to let it out of her sight. Quin deserved recognition, and she was thrilled the research team had honored him.

No wonder the director had been so insistent that she join them in Atlanta. Yet Ella was awash with mixed messages.

She thought of Ian, who had been so solicitous. He'd always been a friend to her. Quin had found fault with him at times, but her husband had been prone to finding fault.

Ross had seemed especially grateful for Quin's contribution. Even the director, who could be cold and unemotional at times, had tears in her eyes when she'd presented Ella with the award.

Yet Nancy hadn't mentioned Quin's name at the medical symposium. Perhaps she had saved her praise until the evening function to make the award more of a surprise.

Ella thought back over the last weeks of Quin's life. The comments he'd made concerning the treatment data played over in her mind. Something had bothered him. If only he would have been more forthcoming.

Zach coughed. She turned to glance at him. Even in the half-light from the car console, she could see that his face was flushed and a line of sweat rimmed his brow.

"Are you feeling okay?" The doctor in her became alert to the signs of some medical problem.

"I'm fine."

She touched his forehead and then pulled his hand to her cheek. "That's strange."

"I don't have a fever," he insisted.

"Maybe not, but something is making you flushed. Do you want me to drive?"

He shook his head. "We're almost to the Freemont turn-off from the highway."

"How's your stomach?"

He shrugged. "A bit queasy."

"The twins had a gastrointestinal virus the night of the attack. You could have been exposed at the clinic."

"The twins were gone by the time I arrived."

"Still, if you'd touched the bedding or if the virus lingered in the air... That type of bug is highly contagious."

"I don't have a stomach bug. It's probably fatigue." He rubbed his brow.

"You've got a headache?"

"A dull one, but nothing I can't handle."

"Men always try to be so strong."

He glanced at her with tired eyes.

"I didn't mean that as a negative comment," she was quick to add. "But it's the truth, Zach. I want you to lie down in my treatment room when we get to the clinic. You can't drive back to Fort Rickman tonight."

"I planned to stay at Tyler's house."

"You don't want him to get sick," she reasoned.

"He's out of town."

"As ill as you look, you shouldn't be alone. Are you sure you don't want me to drive?"

He shook his head again. "Here's the turnoff. We'll be at your clinic before long."

The drive through Freemont and then onto the road to the Amish community seemed to take longer than usual tonight.

Ella didn't like the way Zach looked. His face was pasty white and his breathing seemed labored. He held the steering wheel with one hand and rubbed his stomach with the other. A twenty-four hour virus was the most logical diagnosis, but she'd know more when she got him into her clinic and took his vitals.

Whatever was affecting him, it wasn't good.

"Turn there," she suggested. "It's a shortcut."

He shook his head. "I want to drive by the Landers place to make sure the twins and their grandmother are safe."

"Can you ever stop being a special agent caring for the needs of others?" Ella asked, hearing the sharpness in her tone, no doubt from worry.

"It's my job," he answered.

A job that was taking a toll on him, especially tonight.

He pulled the car into the Landerses' driveway. Ella grabbed his arm when he started to get out. "Stay here," she insisted. "I'll run to the door and talk to Lucy."

She hated to leave him. "Are you sure you can make it to the clinic?"

He nodded. "Just see if the Landerses are all right."

Ella hurried to the door and tapped lightly so as not to wake the girls. "Mrs. Landers?"

"Who's there?" The grandmother's worried voice came from inside the house.

"It's Dr. Jacobsen."

The older woman opened the door, her face tight with

concern. "Bob called. He said he saw you in Atlanta. He was surprised that you were attending the charity event."

"And I was surprised to see him. Are the girls all right?"

"They're fine."

"Did you or anyone else get the virus?"

"Thankfully, no, but then my husband always says I'm healthy as an ox."

Ella had to smile. "With everything that's happened, keep your doors locked. Corporal Powers is supposed to remain on post tonight. If he happens to knock at your door, call the police. Don't let him in. He's going through a hard time and needs to remain under observation."

"Sergeant Abrams called and told me to use caution. I hate to hear bad things about my son-in-law, but the officer reminded me that the twins' safety is the most important thing."

Relieved, Ella hurried back to the car. When she opened the door, she knew something was very wrong with Zach.

"You need to go to the hospital," she insisted.

He shook his head. "You're a doctor. I'm in good hands."

Ever the optimist and always affirming.

When they arrived at her clinic, Zach was nauseous and could hardly climb the steps to the porch. Unlocking the door, Ella noticed a note stuck under the mat.

"It's from Levi." She read the hastily written script. *"Sarah wants to visit her sister. We're going to Alabama for the weekend."*

Traveling in a horse-drawn buggy wasn't what she would recommend for a pregnant woman, but Levi could take care of his wife. Ella needed to focus on Zach.

She helped him into a treatment room and had him stretch out on one of the cots. He had a low-grade temperature with an elevated pulse. She gave him an anti-nausea medication and encouraged him to close his eyes.

"The medicine will make you sleepy. That's the best

thing you can do now. When you wake up, you should feel better."

As he drifted to sleep, she thought back again to everything that had happened in Atlanta. The video and the information the director had provided didn't add up. Either the data had been transposed or Ella's memory was faulty.

The first night, Zach had said her husband's death could have something to do with the clinic attack. She'd thought that foolish at the time, but now she realized it could all play together. If only she could find the missing link. The box of Quin's things would be someplace to start.

Thinking of her Amish neighbors and their trust in the Lord, Ella clasped her hands and bowed her head. "Lord, direct my steps. This terrible turn of events needs to stop before someone else is hurt." She looked at Zach, with his flushed face. "Keep Zach in Your care."

Hurrying to the hallway closet, she pulled out a box, rummaged through the contents and found the framed picture of the three sets of Amish twins.

The twins will provide the answer, Quin had said shortly before he left for Memphis.

She turned over the frame. On the back, he had written the dates when the children had started treatment. The Zook twins—two blond-headed boys—were the breakthrough case when Quin first realized they'd developed a successful treatment.

But the director said the Zook twins had come to the clinic three months after Quin had first seen them and two weeks after his death. Ella didn't understand the discrepancy in the dates. Nor did she understand why Ross had forgotten about the two other sets of twins.

Sitting at her desk, she clutched the frame to her heart, wishing she could clear away the confusion. Her fingers touched something wedged under the cardboard backing on the frame. Her pulse raced as she pulled out the staples that held the cardboard in place, and found a tiny flash drive.

With trembling hands, she inserted the device into her computer and opened the file. Pages of data that Quin had saved appeared, information that was supposed to have remained at the Harrisburg Genetic Research Center.

Ella scrolled through the results, her heart pounding. She was close to uncovering whatever had bothered her husband. Perhaps something that led to his death.

At the end of the last page, she read the final paragraph Quin had written. "I'm heading to Memphis this afternoon and am prepared to confront my assistant. The treatment of three sets of twins—the Yoder, Zook and Hershberger children—was mishandled. The protocol that I developed, which provided the fastest and most efficacious treatment, was not given to all the children. One child in each set of twins received a substandard and less effective medication, and those children have suffered serious complications. The mishandling of these three cases is criminal and was, no doubt, done to decrease cost and thus increase profits. I plan to get to the bottom of this problem, find the person at fault and notify the authorities of medical malpractice."

Ella thought back to the garbled voice she'd heard. A British accent. Had Quin's assistant tampered with or switched the medication each child was to receive? Did he know about the data Quin kept, and had he come after Ella in hopes of finding the flash drive?

Ella needed to call the director to warn her. "The data you presented today is inaccurate," Ella said when Nancy answered her cell.

After explaining what she had found on the flash drive, Ella added, "I remember Quin saying that Ian had been involved in the production of a low-cost treatment that had been rejected early on. Maybe Ian made the switch to compare his own product against the one Quin had developed."

"I don't understand."

Ella told her about the break-in and the attack in her clinic. "I called you some months ago and mentioned reading Quin's notes. Ian must have feared that I had information that would reveal his devious scheme to gain recognition."

"You talked to Ian?"

"Only briefly, before he transferred my call to your extension. I kept thinking about what you had said at the symposium, and the photos used for the tribute to Quin. The dates they were taken appeared at the bottom of each photograph. I wrote down the dates you mentioned at the symposium this morning, and they didn't match. The breakthrough case was actually much earlier than you documented. It was when Quin first developed the treatment. Yet the data you used at the symposium—data Ian must have given you—incorrectly noted that the treatment was not developed until after Quin's death. It's Quin's work, yet the team is claiming the breakthrough as their own."

"You're sure about this?" the director asked.

"I've got the flash drive that has everything on it."

"Thank you, Ella. I've been suspicious that something underhanded may have been going on. I'll call Security here at the hotel to apprehend Ian."

"Be careful, Nancy. The person who came after me was armed and dangerous. Quin didn't take his own life. I'm convinced Ian killed him."

"He'll be arrested within the hour. Keep this confidential until he's apprehended. I wouldn't want anything to undermine the charity work that was done tonight. And again, thank you for being with us and for all Quin did for the research team."

Ella hung up, relieved that everything was coming to

an end and that the truth about Quin's death would soon be revealed.

"Ella?" Zach's voice sounded weak.

"Are you okay?" She hurried to the treatment room.

His face was beet red, and he was gasping for air. "I... can't...breathe..."

She grabbed a syringe and a vial of epinephrine. "You're having some type of allergic reaction."

Had he inadvertently eaten seafood?

She filled the syringe, tied a tourniquet around his left arm and started to inject the medication.

A noise sounded behind her. Before she could release the tourniquet and completely dispense the epinephrine, someone grabbed her shoulders.

She screamed and fought against his hold. The syringe dropped from her hand.

Zach struggled off the cot and threw himself against the man who held her bound. The guy punched Zach in the chest. He doubled over, wheezing. His legs buckled, and he fell to the floor. His head hit the hard tile.

"No!" Ella threw her arms back against the assailant and kicked her legs. "He needs the rest of the injection or he'll die."

"You will, too," her captor snarled. "On the wooden bridge not far from here. You'll die like your husband." His hand tightened around her neck. "Where's the flash drive?" he demanded.

"I'll never tell you."

He cursed and struck her head. She cried in pain and struggled to get free.

"You can't get away with this, Ian."

"You're not even smart enough to know your killer."

She jerked, trying to see his face, but he held her tight against his chest and started to drag her out of the clinic.

They passed a glass-fronted cabinet containing medical supplies. She saw her own reflection in the glass.

Narrowing her gaze, she gasped, never expecting to see the face of the man who wanted to kill her.

"Ross!"

Zach dug his way back from oblivion and gasped for air. He'd heard Ross and knew the bridge he mentioned. Fall rains had raised the water level. Ella wouldn't—couldn't—survive in the angry current. Zach's heart pounded and his pulse raced. He had to save her.

After rolling to his side, he pushed himself upright. A red rash covered his hands and arms, and a metallic taste filled his mouth.

The syringe lay on the floor nearby, more than half filled with medication. The little bit he had received had opened his airway somewhat. Still, he labored to breathe.

Needing to inject the rest, he reached for the syringe, fumbling as he tried to grasp the slick plastic barrel. His fingers were stiff and swollen, the back of his hands splotched with hives.

Angry with his own clumsiness, he willed his limbs to work. Ever so slowly, he grasped the barrel and lifted the syringe off the floor. The tourniquet was still tight around his left arm. Blood seeped from the initial injection site.

Using his right hand, he held the syringe over his vein. His vision blurred. He blinked it back into focus, feeling light-headed as a wave of vertigo swept over him.

Determined to remain conscious, he clamped down on his jaw, slid the needle into his vein and pushed in the plunger. Heat coursed up his arm.

He thought of his mother who had died from an allergy treatment that should have saved her life.

Would the injection do harm or good? He'd know soon enough.

Please, God, help me survive so I can save Ella.

NINETEEN

Buried alive.

That's how Ella felt, locked in the trunk of Ross's car. She forced down the panic that overwhelmed her and focused on getting free.

Ross was driving fast—too fast—over unpaved back roads. Her head crashed against the floor of the trunk with every bump and pothole. Lying in a fetal position as she was, her legs were crammed against her chest. Using her hands and feet, she pushed against the top of the trunk. If only it would open.

What had she seen on television about disengaging the wiring in the taillights to alert law enforcement?

She dug at the carpet that covered the floor and walls of the space where she was confined. Feeling a raw edge, she yanked with all her might. A portion of carpet lifted. She jammed her hand into what felt like a web of wires and tugged on anything that would pull free.

The car slowed to a stop.

Her heart lurched. Had Ross heard her?

She needed a plan.

Think. Think.

When he opened the trunk, she would kick him with both feet. He'd be thrown off guard long enough for her to crawl out and run to safety.

Zach's face played through her mind. He was dying at her clinic. Hot tears burned her eyes, but she couldn't cry. Not now. Nothing could interfere with her getting away from Ross. Only then would she be able to return to her clinic and save Zach.

Footsteps sounded on the gravel roadway.

Ella pulled in a deep breath.

The trunk opened. She kicked, catching Ross's chin. He gasped and took a step backward.

She scrambled out of the trunk, but he grabbed her before she could run.

"You deserve to die," he screamed, and slapped her face. "You're like your husband. He never cared about anyone on the team. He insulted us with his put-downs and negativity."

She fought against Ross's hold. "You tested your own treatment protocol on three children. Quin's was effective, and yours wasn't."

He snarled in rage. "Mine was cheaper. Cutting cost is as important as rapid recovery."

"Not when you're dealing with children's lives." She clawed at his face.

Incensed, he seized her hands. "No one died except Quin. You will, too. People saw you leave the ballroom, upset by the video. They know how distraught you've been since your husband's death."

"Distraught because I knew he didn't take his own life."

Ross wrapped his fingers about her neck. "They'll think you've taken your life just the way he did. That's true love, to follow your husband into death."

Unable to breathe, she jerked a hand free from his grasp and reached for his eyes. He slapped her once, twice, knocking her to the road. Gravel cut her knees and hands. She crawled away from him on all fours. He kicked her. Air whooshed from her lungs, and she gasped with pain.

He kicked her again and again.

Unable to gain her footing, Ella curled into a ball.

She'd rather be beaten to death than die in the water. At least the police would know she hadn't taken her own life.

Grabbing her wrists, Ross pulled her hands behind her back. Pain seared through her arms and up her neck. "No!"

He dragged her over the gravel. The rough rocks scraped against her legs. She lost a shoe. Something sharp cut her foot.

"Help," she screamed, knowing there was no one to hear her. She wouldn't give up, not until every breath was taken from her.

Nearing the side of the bridge, he wrapped his left arm around her waist and shoved her against the guard-rail. The glare from the headlights of his car blinded her. She heard the rush of water and looked down at the dark swell of the raging river.

A cry welled up within her, a plea so forceful it was as if her entire being was focused on three words that circled through her mind, words from scripture she remembered from her youth.

Save me, Lord.

The sound of an oncoming car made Ross hesitate and gave her the motivation to keep fighting. Ella kicked her feet and connected with his shin.

He groaned, trying to lift her over the railing. She threw her head back, crashing against his nose. She made her body go limp, her dead weight forcing him off balance.

The sound of a car engine grew louder. Someone was coming to rescue her, but would he arrive in time?

Zach's head pounded and his eyes blurred. He was driving wildly and riding the middle yellow line, but no one else was on the road tonight. Levi was in Alabama, and Tyler was out of town. Zach had to rely on his own wherewithal. He had called Abrams. Two squad cars were on their way from Freemont, but they wouldn't arrive in time.

His hives had subsided somewhat, but his fingers were still swollen, and his mouth was as dry as cotton. At least his throat was less constricted and he could breathe.

Ross had mentioned the wooden bridge over the river. Zach took the shortcut along the dirt road that wound close to the Fisher home. The bridge stood at least fifteen feet above the river. If Ross hurled Ella into the water, she wouldn't survive. The current was strong and would quickly wash her body downstream.

Rounding a curve in the road, Zach spied headlights ahead. Accelerating, he raced to the bridge, screeched to a stop and leaped from his car. Still woozy, he stumbled toward the crazed researcher who was trying to shove Ella over the railing.

Tackling Ross with one hand, he grabbed Ella with the other. She collapsed to the ground as he punched Ross in the gut. The guy hit back. Zach deflected the blow and struck him again and again.

Ross pulled out a Glock.

Ella screamed.

Zach lunged for the gun. The two men dropped and rolled, fighting for control of the weapon. Zach's eyes blurred, and a roar filled his ears. His grip weakened.

Ross angled the gun at his head.

Amassing the last of his strength, Zach twisted his opponent's wrist a fraction of a second before the researcher pulled the trigger. A round exploded. Ross grabbed his gut and twitched with pain, then let out a dying gasp, and his body went limp.

"Zach," Ella screamed. "Are you all right? Talk to me!"

But he couldn't respond. He didn't have the strength. Ella was alive. That was all that mattered.

TWENTY

Ella turned at the sound of a car approaching on the far side of the bridge.

"Help!" She ran toward the oncoming vehicle and flailed her arms.

A late-model sedan braked to a stop. She gasped with relief. The driver's door opened, and a woman stepped to the pavement.

"Nancy?"

The director held a gun and aimed it at Ella. "Did you plan to escape? Don't you know that we need to get rid of you? Your husband proved to be a problem, and we got rid of him."

"You're working with Ross?"

Nancy didn't realize that her partner in crime was either dying or already dead, and Ella wouldn't be the bearer of bad news.

"Don't you see that our research and the work we do is more important than one man's life?" the director explained. "Quin stood in the way of us finding the most cost-effective treatment. He was convinced his own protocol was best."

"But it was," Ella countered.

"Only we needed to hold on to our capital, so we could

help more children. If Quin had worked with us instead of against us, he would still be alive."

"He knew you were hurting children with subpar treatment."

"And he was so insistent that his protocol was the way to go. We eventually came to that same conclusion, but at a later time."

"After you killed him."

The woman shrugged, as if taking Quin's life had been inconsequential. "Now you're forcing me to kill you, Ella." She glanced around. "Where's Ross?"

Ella refused to answer.

The director's gaze narrowed as she glanced at where the researcher lay. "Is he dead?"

"Turn yourself in, Nancy."

"Absolutely not. All the better if I don't have to worry about Ross. He was always the weak link."

She was even more despicable than Ella had first realized. "You won't get away with this, Nancy. The police will be here in a few minutes."

"I'll say the special agent shot you and Ross, and make it look like you were out to do us harm."

Ella saw movement from the corner of her eye. Relief swept over her. Zach's eyes were open, and his hand was reaching for Ross's gun.

She needed to distract the director. "You sent Ross to my clinic to kill me."

"You said you weren't attending the symposium and charity dinner. But we knew you had information from your husband's data, records that should have remained at the research center. That was so like Quin, thinking he could bend the rules to fit his own needs."

"Someone pushed me onto the MARTA train tracks."

"Yet your boyfriend saved you," the director snarled. "You're like a cat with nine lives. Ross was a fool. He attacked the wrong person in your clinic, then tried to kill you a number of ways, including using his grandfather's rifle. He had hoped feigning an accent would throw you off track. Eventually, he decided the best plan was an anaphylactic reaction. He asked the hotel chef to add a light seafood glaze to the entrées served to the head tables. A glaze that was undetectable, but deadly for anyone allergic to shellfish."

The director's gaze narrowed. "But you didn't eat anything except your salad. We couldn't let you come back to your clinic and piece together the information. When you called about the flash drive, I was already en route here."

"You'll never find the data."

"If necessary, I'll burn down the clinic to get rid of the evidence."

Ella inched her way slowly around the front of the car. She put her hand behind her back and held up three fingers, not even sure if Zach could see them or if he would understand her plan.

Please, God, let this work, she silently prayed.

The director continued to talk about what she'd been able to accomplish and the children who had been helped through the research center.

"Your husband almost ruined all of that, Ella."

She held up two fingers behind her back.

"He was a good researcher, but he was expendable," Nancy continued.

One finger.

Pulling in a breath, Ella pointed behind the director's head and screamed, "Watch out!"

The woman turned, startled, expecting to see someone behind her.

Ella dropped to the ground and scooted to the far side of the car.

Half lying, half sitting, Zach raised Ross's weapon. "Drop your gun! CID Fort Rickman," he cried.

The director turned back and fired wide.

Grasping the weapon with two hands, Zach aimed and fired. The shot made its mark. The gun fell from Nancy's hands. She gasped, clutched her side and collapsed onto the road.

Ella scurried around the car, grabbed the director's gun and felt for her carotid artery. No pulse. She opened Nancy's jacket and began CPR.

Sirens screamed, and police sedans followed by two ambulances screeched to a stop on the bridge.

"We've got it from here, Doc." Two EMTS took over the compressions and worked to keep the director alive.

Ella ran to where Zach sat propped against the bridge. He tried to stand. "Don't get up. You're still dizzy," she told him. She waved over another team of paramedics. "This man needs medical attention."

They quickly got Zach onto a stretcher and lifted him into one of the ambulances. "You're not going without me," she said, climbing in behind them. "I'm his physician."

"Yes, ma'am."

Ella sat on the side seat next to the stretcher.

"I'm okay, Ella," Zach told her.

"Maybe, but we'll let the ER docs decide. And we're heading to the hospital at Fort Rickman."

"It's farther," he said.

"But they're not short staffed."

Ella couldn't let down her guard; she had to stay in control until she knew Zach was receiving the medical care he needed.

The ER doctor was waiting when the ambulance arrived. He raced alongside the stretcher, asking questions, as the medical team rushed Zach into the trauma room.

"You need to wait in the hallway, ma'am." One of the nurses closed the door, shutting Ella out.

Standing in the corridor, not knowing if Zach would be all right, was one of the hardest things Ella had ever had to do. She called Sergeant Abrams to fill him in, and was surprised by the information he shared.

When the door opened and the doctor invited her into the trauma room, she had to hold back tears of relief. Zach still lay on the stretcher, but his color had returned and he was smiling. She even saw a twinkle in his eyes.

"I'm not sure of everything that happened," the ER doc said. "But his symptoms point to histamine fish poisoning."

Ella nodded in agreement. "I talked to the police. Evidently a number of people at the head tables of a banquet we were at fell ill, eating entrées covered with a seafood glaze. The doctors in Atlanta called it scombroid food poisoning, which coincides with your diagnosis."

"How 'bout explaining what it is to the patient?" Zach asked.

"Basically, it's caused by spoiled fish," Ella told him. "Bacteria breaks down protein in the fish and high levels of histamines are the by-product, which causes illness. Although usually not as severe as your reaction, Zach. Public health people in Atlanta are inspecting the hotel kitchen, but the problem could have occurred when the seafood was first shipped to market."

"Special Agent Swain mentioned his mother's allergy to shellfish," the ER doc added. "I'd recommend testing. An allergic reaction could have played into his quite significant response. In either case, the epinephrine helped to open his airway."

Ella was puzzled. "But I only administered a half cc at most."

"I injected myself." Zach held up his left arm and showed her the vein where a large hematoma had formed.

"My advice," the doctor said, "is to keep an EpiPen on hand." Turning to Ella, he added, "We want Special Agent Swain to stay here until his blood pressure returns to normal. If the lab work comes back without question, we'll release him in a few hours and you can take him home."

When the ER doctor left the trauma room, Ella stepped toward the stretcher and leaned over Zach. "I thought I'd lost you. You could hardly breathe, and I knew you were in severe distress."

"I feared Ross would hurl you off the bridge. You can't swim—isn't that what I heard?"

"I'm planning to take lessons."

"A good idea." He touched her cheek and wrapped her hand in his. "You're very brave, Dr. Jacobsen, and very smart."

"And you're always quick with praise." She smiled. "Which is so...well, affirming. I'm thanking God that both of us survived."

"I'm sorry about Quin."

She nodded. "At least I know now that he didn't take his own life. Somehow it's easier to accept, this way, although it only shows how twisted the director and Ross were."

"Do you have any word on Nancy's condition?"

"I told you I called the police when I was in the hallway. Sergeant Abrams said she's critical, but will probably survive."

"And stand trial. What about Ross?"

Ella shook her head. "But there is good news. I asked one of the nurses to call ICU about Mary Kate's condition."

"Tell me she's better."

"How'd you guess? The RN told me she's turned a corner and is expected to make a full recovery. Her husband was with her."

"A lot has happened since that first night at your clinic." Zach touched Ella's hair and weaved a strand around his finger. "But in all the headache and struggle, something good occurred."

"Oh?"

"I got to know a wonderful physician who treats sick kids and makes them better."

"But I almost lost you."

"That wasn't your fault." He hesitated a moment. "I know you're grieving for your husband, but I hope someday you'll find room in your heart to love again."

"I don't think that will be a problem, especially if you're talking about a special agent who saved my life about—" Ella glanced up and pursed her lips coyly "—hmm, maybe four or five times. I'd say that's the type of guy I want to keep around."

"I'd like to stay around." He pulled her closer. "For a long time."

Then she lowered her lips to his, and he did what she'd wanted him to do since the first night they'd met. He kissed her. His kiss was extra sweet.

With a contented sigh, Zach wrapped his arms around her and pulled her even closer. Then he kissed her again and again.

Pulling back ever so slightly, she wiggled her nose and smiled. "As a physician, I need to warn you."

"About what?" he asked.

"Kissing could cause your blood pressure to rise."

"But mine was too low." He feigned wide-eyed innocence. "Which means kissing would be good for the patient."

She laughed. "Good for the doctor, too."

As they waited for the lab tests to be run so Zach could

be released, Ella snuggled against him. She never wanted to leave his embrace. So much had happened that had brought them together, and wrapped in Zach's arms was where she wanted to stay for a very long time.

EPILOGUE

Ella opened the oven, and inhaled the rich aroma as she basted the turkey with butter one last time. Then she glanced at the clock and wiped her hands on a towel. Everyone would arrive soon.

"I'm impressed." Wendy, her nurse, stood nearby and shook her head in amazement. "You're cooking your first Thanksgiving turkey for all these people?"

"I wanted to share the day with special friends. Thanks for joining us and for coming early to help."

After stepping into the dining room, Ella checked the table and admired the flower arrangement Zach had delivered ahead of time. The bouquet of mums and daisies interspersed with roses was gorgeous.

A tap at the entry caused her to giggle with excitement when she saw his car parked outside. "Happy Thanksgiving," she said, opening the door.

"Don't you look beautiful." Zach kissed her lightly on the lips as he stepped inside. Once she'd closed the door, he pulled her into his arms and kissed her again, much more decidedly.

Her toes tingled, and she had a hard time pulling out of his embrace. "Wendy's in the kitchen," she finally teased, alerting him that they weren't alone.

"You're blushing." His eyes twinkled with mischief. "She's seen us kiss before."

"And I hope she sees us kissing many more times."

"Yes, ma'am." He gave her a mock salute. "I can make that happened."

Ella laughed and peered into a shopping bag he carried. "What did you bring?"

"Sodas and sparkling water, and some cheese and crackers to put out before the turkey's ready."

"Perfect." She motioned him into the kitchen. "Wendy can get those ready if you'll move some more chairs around the table."

The rest of the guests arrived and filled the house with merriment and laughter. When the food was ready, Ella invited everyone into the dining room, and Zach carried the turkey to the table.

Levi and a very pregnant Sarah sat across from Tyler and his fiancée. Their Amish neighbors, Isaac and Ruth Lapp, also pregnant and soon to deliver, sat on the far end with their son, Joseph. His blond hair and big blue eyes reminded Ella of the Zook twins, who had been the breakthrough case for CED. A new director had taken over the Harrisburg Genetic Research Center, and Ian was one of the lead physicians on staff.

Zach carved the turkey while Ella and Wendy brought the other dishes to the table. Sweet potato casserole, mashed potatoes, cranberry relish, summer squash and an array of breads, that Sarah had baked, filled the room with even more delicious smells.

"I'd like two helpings of everything," little Joseph said, his eyes wide and a smile on his sweet lips.

"Joseph, you are growing so big now," his mother chimed in. "But you need to eat one plateful of food before you ask for more."

"It looks so *gut, Mamm*."

Ella appreciated the boy's compliment and the artful way his mother had used affirmation to build up her son before she corrected him.

Glancing at Zach, Ella thought of the many times he had affirmed her, which was so opposite from Quin. Sarah's father had been faint on praise, as well. Concerned about the older man, she leaned closer to her neighbor.

"Sarah, have you heard from your father?" she asked.

"*Yah*, we received a letter. He is happy living in Alabama with my sister, and even his health is better. My sister said he is taking the medicine you prescribed."

"I'm glad. What about your brother?"

"He is working for my brother-in-law to pay off the debts he owed. There is a widow with a young child who lives nearby. She has been a good influence on Daniel."

Levi took Sarah's hand and smiled lovingly at his wife. He and Mr. Landers had reconciled their relationship, and Levi had had an opportunity to see the twins before Mary Kate and Hugh moved to his new military assignment at Fort Riley, Kansas.

The guests passed their plates, and Ella filled them high with the delectable assortment of food. Before they started to eat, Zach tapped his water glass to get everyone's attention.

"Ella asked me to say a few words of thanks. She and I consider all of you a blessing in our lives. Levi and Sarah are wonderful neighbors, and it won't be long until their baby is here."

"A very healthy baby," Ella said from her seat next to Sarah. "Why don't you tell them, Levi?"

"Dr. Ella got the results of the DNA tests not long ago. Our baby will be born healthy, without any of the genetic diseases we worried about."

"And on that happy note, let's bow our heads in prayer," Zach said. "Father, God, we thank You for Ella coming

South to open her clinic, and for all that has brought us together on this special day. Thank You for the land across the street that I was able to purchase and for Levi agreeing to help me farm the property. Thank You for Amish friends, and bless Tyler and Carrie as they prepare for their wedding. God bless this food and those who prepared it."

He glanced up and smiled at Ella, causing her to blush with gratitude.

"And thank You for new beginnings," Zach continued. "For affirmation and love, for peaceful settings and for all Your blessings. Especially those we love who are here with us today. Amen."

Everyone ate their fill and then lingered at the table over dessert. Although Joseph had only one helping of the main course, he found room for two slices of pie.

After the guests left, Zach washed the dishes while Ella put everything away. Once the kitchen was tidy, they walked into the living room to the window that looked out upon the land Zach had bought.

"I don't want to rush you," he said, "but I'm feeling overjoyed today and so very grateful."

She nodded and rested her head on his shoulder as they both gazed at the rolling fields and the falling twilight.

"You're all I ever wanted in life, Ella, and I'm so thankful to have found you."

"I feel the same way, Zach. Being with you brings me total joy and happiness that I want to have continue for as long as I live."

He drew her closer. "Then maybe I'm not being too impatient."

He dug in his pocket and pulled out a small box. "I know you needed time, but I hope we've waited long enough. You'll have a lot of details to plan, so we won't be rushing into anything too quickly, but…"

He looked expectantly at her.

"But what?" she asked, her lips twitching in a coy smile.

"Will you marry me and become my wife?"

"I thought you'd never ask." She wrapped her arms around his neck. "Yes, I want to be your wife, and I'll go around the world with you, wherever you're stationed."

"How about right here? I'll get out of the army in another year. Levi can teach me how to farm. We can expand our property and, hopefully, have a family. I can help with the management and upkeep of the clinic, while you treat the children who need your care."

"Oh, Zach, that would make me so happy, but I'd be happy anyplace with you."

"I love you, Ella, and I always will."

"God knew what He was doing when He brought us together," she reasoned.

"That's why He's God," Zach said, before he kissed her again.

Twilight settled over the land and the stars twinkled overhead. A moon glowed in the night sky and showered the earth with shimmering light. Zach and Ella moved onto the front porch and sat wrapped in an Amish quilt, watching the moon rise even higher over the horizon.

Nestled together, they talked about their future, about the children they prayed God would give them and about their life together, joined by love and surrounded by the beauty of God's bounty. Freemont, Georgia, and this Amish community would be their home, where they would raise their family and, with God's blessing, live happily ever after.

* * * * *

Discover the rest of the MILITARY INVESTIGATIONS series by Debby Giusti by picking up

Dear Reader,

I hope you enjoyed *Plain Truth*, the tenth book in my Military Investigations series, which features heroes and heroines in the army's Criminal Investigation Division. Each story stands alone, so you can read them in any order, either in print or as an ebook: *The Officer's Secret*, book 1; *The Captain's Mission*, book 2; *The Colonel's Daughter*, book 3; *The General's Secretary*, book 4; *The Soldier's Sister*, book 5; *The Agent's Secret Past*, book 6; *Stranded*, book 7; *Person of Interest*, book 8; and *Plain Danger*, book 9.

Pediatrician Ella Jacobsen never expects that opening her Children's Care Clinic in the heart of Amish country, near Freemont, Georgia, will land her in the middle of a criminal investigation. But someone is after the pretty doctor, only she doesn't know why. CID Special Agent Zach Swain tries to keep her safe…and alive. Zach holds a grudge against the medical profession, and the last thing Ella wants is to fall in love. The odds are stacked against them until they put their faith in God.

I want to hear from you. Email me at debby@debbygiusti. com or write me c/o Love Inspired, 195 Broadway, 24th Floor, New York, NY 10007. Visit my website at www.DebbyGiusti. com, blog with me at www.seekerville.blogspot.com and at www.crossmyheartprayerteam.blogspot.com, and friend me at www.facebook.com/debby.giusti.9.

As always, I thank God for bringing us together through this story.

Wishing you abundant blessings,
Debby

COMING NEXT MONTH FROM
Love Inspired® Suspense

Available October 4, 2016

LISCNM0916

Deputy Sheriff Audrey Martin sang along with the
Christmas carol playing on the patrol-car radio. The radio
crackled and buzzed before the sheriff's department
dispatcher, Ophelia Leighton, came on the line. "Unit
one, do you copy?"

Thumbing the answer button, Audrey replied, "Yes,
Dispatch, I copy."

"Uh, there's a reported sighting of a—"

The radio crackled and popped. In the background,
Audrey heard Ophelia talking, then the deep timbre of
the sheriff's voice. "Uh, sorry about that." Ophelia came
back on the line. "We're getting mixed reports, but
bottom line there's something washed up on the shore of
the Pine Street beach."

"Something?" Audrey shifted the car into Drive and
took off toward the north side of town. "What kind of
something?"

"Well, one report said a beached whale," Ophelia
came back with. "Another said dead shark. But a couple
people called in to say a drowned fisherman."

Her heart cramped with sorrow for the father she'd lost so many years ago to the sea.

She brought her vehicle to a halt in the cul-de-sac next to an early-model pickup truck where a small group of gawkers stood, and she climbed out.

"Audrey." Clem Previs rushed forward to grip her sleeve, his veined hand nearly blue from the cold. "Shouldn't you wait for the sheriff?"

Pressing her lips together, she covered Clem's hand with hers. "Clem, I can handle this," she assured him.

About ten yards down the beach, a man dressed from head to toe in black and wearing a mask that obscured his face struggled to drag something toward the water's edge.

Audrey narrowed her gaze. Her pulse raced. Amid a tangle of seaweed and debris, she could make out the dark outline of a large body. She shivered with dread. That certainly wasn't a fish, whale or shark. Definitely human. And from the size, she judged the body to be male.

And someone was intent on returning the man to the ocean.

Don't miss
IDENTITY UNKNOWN by Terri Reed,
available wherever
Love Inspired® Suspense books and ebooks are sold.

www.LoveInspired.com